R.L. THORTON

Bi the Way

First edition

ISBN: 978-1-0689743-1-1

Editing by Ayesha E.B.
Proofreading by Leona K.
Cover art by Margaux G.

This book was professionally typeset on Reedsy.
Find out more at reedsy.com

To my Aunt Leona.
Without all your hard work, this book wouldn't have been possible.
Thank you.

Contents

I

Part One

1

Maybe

Sunburned and sandy, 14-year-old Rodney Thompson trudged up the driveway after a day at the beach with Zain, only to be confronted by an unwelcome sight: a "For Sale" sign planted firmly in their front lawn. He rubbed his eyes, praying he was seeing things but the sign didn't vanish. He burst through the front door and found his mom, Sasha, talking to a sharply dressed realtor in the living room.

"Mom? What's going on?" Rodney stammered, his voice cracking with distress.

Sasha glanced at the realtor before turning to her son. "Rodney, I got a new job as head nurse at Strathroy Memorial Hospital. I know this is short notice, but the job starts September 1st."

"Strathroy?" Rodney echoed, feeling as if the floor had just dropped out from beneath him. Where the hell was Strathroy, it didn't even sound like a real place.

"Look, living in the city has become too expensive, and the hospital is demanding longer hours with no overtime pay," she explained, her voice firm and resolute. "Taking this job is the best thing for our family right now."

"But… this is our home; this is where Dad was with us." Rodney's sensitive brown eyes brimmed with unshed tears, his voice barely audible.

"Rodney, things change, and we have to adapt" Sasha replied, her tone bordering on harsh. "It's just a house. I have to do what is best for us."

Without another word, Rodney went to his room, slamming the door behind him. He threw himself onto his bed, looking around at all the photos of his dad and him on their many adventures throughout the city. He could feel his tears building again, staring at his father's old guitar in the corner. That's when he heard his sister Marcy's gentle knock on the door.

"Rod, Mom doesn't want to leave either," Marcy said softly, her voice muffled by the barrier between them. "But this job means she can finally rest without worrying about the bills piling up. You know, ever since Dad died last year, she hasn't done anything but work. I don't even think she has really processed it herself."

"I know," Rodney muttered under his breath, the weight of his sister's words hung heavy on his heart. She was right after all, their mom had been working overtime to keep the house, not to mention the cost of his vocal and guitar lessons or Marcy's dance competitions. Rodney couldn't even remember a time he saw his mom shed a tear since the funeral.

"Just give it a try, please, for Mom," Marcy asked, her tone soft but serious.

Rodney took a breath, "OK, I will try," but he failed to even convince himself.

A week later, Rodney found himself squished into the backseat of their packed car, watching Toronto recede in the rear-view mirror. As the Thompsons hit the road, he couldn't help but worry about starting a million kilometres away from all his friends. He wondered if Strathroy would even have a music store, ever since his dad passed away all he wanted to do was learn to play the guitar like him, his best friend Ally said he was getting better. He wondered if Ally ever got any of his text messages, she was on vacation with her family and never texted him back. All his uncertainty made his stomach hurt as his old home faded from view.

———-

They pulled up to a small white house on an overgrown corner lot. Both Rodney and Marcy were unimpressed, large weeds sprouted out from the cracks in the driveway. The musty scent of old memories greeted them as they stepped out of the car and gazed upon the discoloured siding of the three-bedroom, two-bathroom house. Rodney shuddered at the thought of just how creepy the basement must be – how could he ever bring his new friends here?

"Maybe it won't be so bad on the inside," Rodney mused, trying to convince himself more than anyone else. "After all, mom did say it was charming."

"Exactly," Marcy agreed, her freckled face glowing with optimism. "And besides, paint was invented for a reason, right?"

"Exactly," Rodney nodded as they ventured up the crumbling steps to the door. The red peeling door opened into a narrow entranceway with a small closest.

"Before you go any farther take off your shoes," Their mother called from the car. "Rodney your room is down the hall second door on the left and Marcy yours is at the very end of the hall. All your boxes should be in your rooms."

"Thanks, mom," Rodney said with a small smile. He made his way through the cramped dining room and into the hall, counting the doors until he got to his new room.

Inside his new room, Rodney squinted at the paisley wallpaper glued to his room's walls. His imagination trying to add shelves for his soccer trophies and oceanic figures. He stood there, lost in thought when his phone vibrated in his pocket. Ally's name glowed across the screen.

"Hey, Ally!" Rodney greeted, his face lighting up as he answered the FaceTime call from his best friend. "I didn't think you'd be able to talk so soon. Didn't your plane just land?"

"OMG, Rodney!" Ally said, her long blonde hair falling in front of her sparkling blue eyes. "We just got back into the country, and I got all of your texts. I can't believe you moved away, Rodney! High school won't be the same without you." Ally's mom was a big-time author and they had gone to Paris over the summer so she could write her latest romance novel.

"Trust me, I feel the same way," he sighed, running a hand through his short brown hair. "I don't know how I'm going to survive small-town life. At least you still have Zain,"

"Hey, don't worry about the small-town thing," Ally said reassuringly. "You'll make new friends and show them all how smart you are. And who knows? Maybe I'll come visit sometime."

"Really?" The idea of Ally visiting him in Strathroy brightened his day considerably. "That would be amazing."

"Definitely." She smiled, and Rodney felt his heart flutter. "Stay strong, okay? You're going to do great. I miss you already."

"Miss you too," Rodney started before Ally's brother called her to come get her bags.

"Well, that is my queue," Ally said flashing Rodney a smile that made his heart melt. "Seriously, I can't wait to hear everything about your new high school on Monday. It is going to be awesome, I just know it."

"Thanks, Ally," he said softly before they said their goodbyes and hung up. A bittersweet feeling washed over him – he wished he had told her how he really felt before he moved away. They had been friends since the first grade, but something changed in seventh grade when Ally jokingly kissed him at a party, it felt like how love was described in every movie.

Pulling his attention away from his phone, Rodney turned his attention back to the room he had been given. The walls were bare, and the carpet was worn, but it was his space. As he began unpacking boxes, he stumbled upon a collection of old photos: renting bikes with friends, hanging out by the waterfront, and going to Blue Jays games with his dad.

The memories tugged at his heart, and he couldn't shake the feeling that he might not have anything in common with anyone at his new school. His thoughts raced, overflowing with anxiety and uncertainty. The night seemed to crawl by, and he decided to skip the Chinese takeout and head to bed early, wondering what his first day of high school would bring.

———-

The morning sun glinted off the orange brick exterior of SDCI, as students stepped off their buses and headed toward the green doors that lined the back of the school. It was an odd colour combination that made the school look like it was carved from a pumpkin. Rodney hesitated for a moment, his imagination making every student's eyes follow him as he made his way toward the door. Most of these kids had gone through school together and knew everything about each other, and Rodney felt like he stuck out like a sore thumb.

"Hey, watch it!" a voice snapped, jolting Rodney back to reality as another student bumped into him. Flushed with embarrassment and anxiety, he hurried through the green doors and found himself in the busy cafeteria. The air buzzed with excited chatter as student volunteers stood at long tables, handing out class schedules.

Rodney's heart pounded in his chest as he scanned the room, finally locating the line for last names ending in T. He shifted nervously from foot to foot as he waited, rehearsing a mental pep talk to get him through the day. At last, it was his turn. "Rodney Thompson," he muttered to the volunteer, who handed him a schedule with a friendly smile.

"First class is Geography with Mrs. Willberry," he read aloud, not exactly his favourite subject. His mouth was dry, and he could practically feel the weight of the unknown pressing down on him. Swallowing hard, Rodney made his way to the classroom and took a seat near the front, hoping to go unnoticed by the crowd of freshmen filing in.

His pulse raced, and he couldn't help but avoid eye contact with his fellow ninth graders. But then as he did a quick scan of the classroom, he spotted something. A familiar face, as if the universe was playing a trick on him.

He took another look up to the door of the classroom, at the girl with the long blonde hair and perfect smile. She looked exactly like Ally, from her small button nose to her worn-out purple Converse. Rodney blinked in disbelief, but she was actually there, in his classroom. It was Ally, the pink boba tea keychain he gave her was dangling from her checker backpack.

"Ally?" he stammered, unable to suppress his shock. She grinned, her blue eyes sparkling as she slid into the empty seat beside him. "What are you doing here!"

"Surprise!" she exclaimed, her smile so genuine it made Rodney blush. "My mom's doing research for her new small-town mystery novel 'Cornfields and Killers', so I may have mentioned the perfect small town for her to do her research in."

"That is amazing!" Rodney said. He wasn't going to be alone in high school after all, his best friend was there to make everything better.

"Well, I couldn't let you face the farmers alone," She joked. "Besides, high school would be no fun at all without you," Ally smiled and Rodney couldn't help but feel as though the universe was finally on his side for a change. His heart swelled with relief and gratitude, his earlier fears melting away in the warmth of her presence.

"Alright, class," Mrs. Willberry called out, bringing everyone's attention to the front. As the lesson began, Rodney struggled to concentrate on anything other than being close to Ally. Her casual touch on his arm sent shivers up his spine, and all he could think about was how he was given a second chance to finally tell Ally how he felt.

Determined not to let this opportunity slip through his fingers, Rodney made a pact with himself: before the end of the school year, he would tell Ally that he wanted to be more than just friends. And as he glanced over at her, stealing a quick glance at her radiant smile, he felt a surge of hope that maybe – just maybe – his new life in Strathroy wouldn't be so bad after all.

2

It's

The first week of school seemed to blow by faster than Rodney ever expected. The bustling cafeteria of SDCI was alive with the sounds of laughter and conversation, but Rodney sat alone at a corner table, picking at his soggy fries, he still felt out of place in the country setting. He imagined the lively group surrounding Ally at lunch and wished he had been lucky enough to have the same lunch period as her. He would've loved to sit next to her as she excitedly discussed yoga poses, from the club she started, with her new friends. Rodney couldn't help but feel envious, wishing he could be part of that circle.

His focus then switched to a group of guys eating at the table next to his and their discussion about the Turkey Festival. "Ugh, it's like they're speaking some alien language," he muttered to himself, pushing his food around the tray. How was it that Ally could just become one with this while he struggled to find his place?

The bell rang and as if on cue, Matt sauntered through the cafeteria, a confident smirk playing on his lips. Rodney's heart sank as he remembered what he saw earlier at the lockers, Matt's arm casually draped around Ally's shoulders. He's flirting with her, thought Rodney, and he was being so obvious about it. Why did Matt have to be so charming?

A static buzz from the intercom broke Rodney's train of thought. The principal's voice echoed through the school's PA system, "Attention students, a reminder that the homecoming committee will be meeting after school today. The theme of this year's dance is pumpkin patch, hope to see you all there." The upcoming dance only stressed Rodney out more.

Rodney knew he wanted to ask Ally, but fate seemed to conspire against him. One day, he tripped over a stray backpack just as he approached her, spilling his books all over the hallway and missing his chance. Another time, he found himself tongue-tied when Ally asked him about his weekend plans. "Oh, uh… well, I was going to… never mind," he stammered, his cheeks flushing bright red. Ally just gave him that warm smile and he seemed to melt right there.

With only two days left before the dance, today was the day he mustered enough courage to ask her to the dance between periods, Ally smiled warmly and said, "Oh… well… I'm actually going with a group of friends, but you should totally join us, Rodney!"

"Sure," he replied with a forced smile, his heart sinking in disappointment. He had hoped for something more than just tagging along. As Ally walked away to her next class, Rodney leaned against the lockers, his thoughts racing. "Why wasn't I clearer?" he scolded himself under his breath. "Well, I guess it's better than nothing."

With each passing day, Rodney couldn't help but wonder why it was so hard to make Ally see him as more than just a childhood friend. He told himself, he'd settle for the chance to hang out with her, even if it meant sharing her attention with Matt.

———-

The gymnasium pulsated with the beat of the music, transforming into a wonderland of twinkling fairy lights and bails of hay with intricately carved pumpkins placed on top of them. Rodney stood at the edge of the group Ally had invited him to join, feeling like an undercover agent infiltrating enemy territory. He watched as Ally twirled and laughed with her friends. The sight of Matt's hand resting on her waist ignited a tiny fire in Rodney's chest.

"Hey, you're Rodney, right?" A voice pulled him from his thoughts. He turned to see Parker, his curly hair bouncing with every movement. "I've seen you around school. I'm in science class with Ally. Parker Evans" He held out his hand.

"Nice to meet you," Rodney replied, taking it and giving it an awkward shake. "I'm actually taking science next semester. With Ms. Sears, apparently, she is very hands-on with science experiments."

"Definitely! We just started learning about genetics with her. It's amazing how all living things are controlled by these tiny bits of mRNA," Parker said, his face lighting up as he spoke.

"Wow, I've never heard of mRNA before. Is it like DNA?" Rodney's own excitement bubbled up, and he found himself drawn into conversation. As they chatted about the intricacies of DNA and chromosomes, Rodney felt a little more at ease now that he wasn't focusing so much on what Ally was doing.

"Hey, we should exchange contact info," Parker suggested, holding out his phone. "We can talk more about science and stuff. I would be nice to have another nerd around here,"

"Sure thing," Rodney agreed, feeling a small victory in making a new friend. They tapped their phones together, sharing their details.

"So, how do you know Ally?" Parker asked curiously.

"Ally and I have known each other since kindergarten," Rodney explained, a nostalgic smile creeping onto his face. "We practically grew up together, did everything together. She's been my best friend for as long as I can remember."

"Wow, that's really sweet," Parker said earnestly. "You're a good friend to her, and she's going to need you now more than ever."

"Wh-what do you mean?" Rodney stammered, caught off guard.

"Because she's dating Matt now," Parker revealed, his voice laced with concern. "He's... well, he can be a bit of a controlling jerk, but he isn't all bad. Like this one time on my 12th birthday, he demanded the theme should be......"

Rodney's heart plummeted, the fire in his chest blazing into an inferno. He barely registered Parker's words about how Matt basically decided his whole birthday for him but then surprised him with the most thoughtful gift ever, an Xbox. His world had narrowed down to one devastating fact: Ally was dating Matt, and she hadn't told him. They had texted back and forth every night and hung out on Saturdays so why would she have kept this detail from him? In his mind, Matt became a fearsome dragon who ensnared Ally in the castle tower.

"Rodney? You okay?" Parker's voice sounded far away, echoing in Rodney's despair.

Rodney shook his head but then corrected it to a nod "Yeah it is just a bit stuffy in here, I am going to get some air." Rodney needed to get out there. He felt like Ally had been lying to him with every text and conversation, hiding her romance, would a best friend do that?

"Oh, no worries I'll come with you," Parker tucked his phone into his pocket but when he looked up, Rodney was gone, swallowed by the dancing crowd in search of solace.

———-

The school garden was his sanctuary, its soft grass and fragrant flowers soothing Rodney's frayed nerves. He sank onto a worn wooden bench, the cool autumn air brushing against his cheeks, and pulled out his phone to distract himself from the nauseous feeling building up inside him. Scrolling through his options, he settled on The Fault in Our Stars, hoping a story about finding love against all odds would give him some hope.

"Hey man, mind if I join you?" A voice interrupted Rodney's escape into the world of Hazel and Augustus. Glancing up, he saw a tall, lean figure standing over him, his friendly smile framed by tousled brown hair. "I'm Derek, I take it the dance isn't your scene either."

"Yeah, I guess not," Rodney muttered, shifting over to make room on the bench. "I'm Rodney."

"Nice to meet you, Rodney." Derek sat down beside him, his eyes drawn to the screen as the movie played on. After a moment, he turned to face Rodney, curiosity tinting his words. "So, why are you out here looking so blue?"

Rodney hesitated, unsure whether he wanted to share his heartache with a near stranger. But something about Derek's easygoing demeanour made him feel weirdly at ease. "I'm in love with my best friend, Ally, but she's dating someone else now. But she didn't tell me she was dating someone else so it feels like this is her way of saying she knows I like her but she doesn't like me,"

"Ah, seems like a convoluted way to say 'Hey, let's just be friends,'" Derek mused. "Hence the depressing romantic movie. But hey, take it from someone who has been here a while, most relationships at SDCI don't last a month. If you really love her, you just have to wait it out."

"Maybe, but I've had feelings for her for years," Rodney confessed, the weight of his secret spilling from his lips. "I was afraid if I told her, it would ruin our friendship. I just feel like the universe is doing everything in its power to play with my heart."

"Man, that's tough," Derek sympathized, resting a hand on Rodney's shoulder. "But maybe it just isn't the right time yet, maybe your epic romance is the end game. I mean who is this prince charming who has won her over anyway?"

"Matt Jenkins," Rodney said flatly, and Derek fell silent. Both teens turned their attention back to the movie, Rodney's thoughts raced, trying to imagine a future where he and Ally could be together. He barely noticed when Derek spoke up again, determination shining in his eyes.

"Listen, Rodney, I'm going to help you win the girl. Everyone deserves their own epic love story, and I'm volunteering to make sure you get yours."

"Really?" Rodney blinked at him, taken aback by the offer. "But we just met."

"Hey, sometimes that's all it takes. Besides, I know Matt and trust me, no one deserves to be with him," Derek grinned, his smile chasing away some of Rodney's doubts. "I know a thing or two about relationships and what makes them work. Trust me, by the end of the semester, she will know exactly who her prince charming really is."

As Hazel and Augustus danced across the screen, Rodney felt a fragile hope begin to bloom in his chest yet again. Maybe, with Derek's help, he could find a way to reach out to Ally, to bridge the gap that had formed between them. And maybe, just maybe, they could write their own love story after all.

3

Ally

Rodney's heart hammered in his chest as he leaned against the lockers, waiting for Derek to arrive. He nervously tapped his fingers on his backpack, lost in thought when Derek suddenly appeared in front of him.

"Hey, Rodney," Derek said with his signature grin, "I've got a plan to win over Ally. But first, we need to know our enemy: Matt. We need to find his weaknesses so we can exploit them."

Rodney furrowed his brow, unsure about the plan. "And how do you propose we do that?"

Derek leaned closer, lowering his voice. "You're going to befriend him. Get close, figure out what makes him tick."

"Are you crazy?" Rodney whispered, glancing around to make sure no one was listening. "He's dating Ally! I can't just… hang out with him."

Derek rolled his eyes. "Come on, Rodney, it's not like you're asking him to prom."

"If it is so easy, why don't you do it?" he asked, doubting his ability to make a friend on command.

"I would, but Matt knows who I am. It has to be you," Before Rodney could protest further, Derek pointed down the hall where Matt and Ally stood, sharing a tender kiss.

Jealousy flared in Rodney's chest, and he clenched his fists. "OK, how are we doing this?"

———-

Later that afternoon, Rodney followed Matt to the weight room, trying to blend in among the other students working out. As he approached a rowing machine, he realized he had no clue what he was doing. He watched others using the equipment, attempting to mimic their movements but only succeeding in looking awkward and uncomfortable.

"Need some help?" Matt's voice came from behind him, startling Rodney. His cheeks flushed red as he turned to face his romantic rival.

"Uh, yeah. I guess, I'm not really used to this stuff," Rodney admitted, forcing a sheepish grin.

"They don't have rowing machines in the big city, eh," Matt said in a tone that made Rodney unsure if it was a joke or not.

"Oh no, I'm just trying a 'new town, new me' thing. I guess it is pretty obvious, I haven't spent much time in a gym before." Rodney admitted

"OK, well let me show you how it works." Matt motioned for Rodney to step aside then he stepped up to the machine, demonstrating how to properly use it.

"Thank you, uh do you mind showing me how to use the other machines too?"

Matt gave Rodney a nod to follow him. As they worked out together, Rodney found himself oddly at ease with Matt. They chatted about classes, sports, and even their favourite TV shows.

Soon Rodney was lost in his imagination, he had found himself in an alien world surrounded by beings he didn't understand. One of the extraterrestrials, however, had taken the time to teach him the ways and he had an appreciation for that. Lost in his own world, Rodney didn't seem to notice that Matt was texting Ally every few minutes.

But Rodney returned to reality as they approached the weight bench, Matt showed him some basic lifting techniques, and Rodney pushed his daydreams aside. This guy was not a helpful alien guiding him through new territory, he was the guy standing between him and the girl he loved.

"Hey Rodney," Matt said as they finished their workout, bringing Rodney's attention back to him, "a few of us are hanging out at the park on Saturday.

You should come."

"Uh, sure," Rodney replied hesitantly, feeling the weight of Derek's plan heavy on his shoulders.

"Great, see you there!" Matt grinned, and they parted ways. As Rodney walked home, he couldn't help but feel conflicted about the whole situation.

He wanted to hate Matt, everyone else seemed to, but he really didn't. He pulled out his phone and texted Derek about the unexpected connection he had made with Matt during their workout.

Derek responded swiftly: "Be careful not to get too attached. I know he comes off as this amazing guy, but under all that charm is the real Matt. He knows how to manipulate people."

Rodney sighed and stuffed his phone back into his pocket. How could he possibly sabotage Matt and Ally's relationship when he was starting to actually like the guy? Was Derek right? Was there something he wasn't seeing? His thoughts churned as he approached his house, only to find Ally waiting for him on his front porch.

"Hey, stranger," she greeted him with a warm smile. "Feels like we haven't had time to talk lately."

"Yeah, it has been a while," Rodney agreed, his heart fluttering. "Want to go grab some dinner at Roy's?"

"Sounds perfect," Ally replied, and they headed off to the diner together.

As they sat in the cozy booth, surrounded by the scent of sizzling burgers and fries, Rodney imagined that they were on a fancy date, complete with candlelight and soft music. Their conversation flowed effortlessly, and he found himself lost in her blue eyes.

"So where have you been? I feel like I only see glimpses of you at school" Ally asked. "Are you busy with clubs or something?"

"Um, I don't really do much," Rodney admitted sheepishly. "I'm still adjusting to everything here."

"Oh, I thought you would have joined the science club by now," Ally suggested. "You've always loved doing your own science experiments. Remember that time you built your own rocket out of pop bottles in grade 1?"

"Oh yeah," Rodney thought back to the mess of a bottle rocket, barely held together with tape, "It got stuck on the school roof on its first launch," he laughed.

"See … the science club does those kinds of experiments all the time, plus Parker is a part of the club and you two seemed to be having a good chat at the dance." Ally pressed.

Rodney considered the idea, but his thoughts were interrupted by the sound of Ally's phone buzzing. She glanced down at the screen, her face lighting up as she read the text from Matt.

"Sorry, I have to go, the boyfriend is calling," she said, slipping out of the booth. "But let me know if you decide to join the club, okay?"

"Sure," Rodney replied, feeling a knot in his stomach as he watched her leave. The imagined fancy date had vanished, replaced by cold reality. It felt like Matt had some secret ability to disrupt his limited time with his best friend. Derek's plan seemed more appealing than ever before in his mind, and he would get his chance to learn more about Matt on Saturday.

———-

The sun dipped low in the sky as Rodney approached Victoria Park on Saturday. He spotted Matt, Parker, Steven, and Jordan sitting together on a cluster of wooden benches, their voices carrying through the air as they laughingly shared stories.

"Rodney! Over here!" Parker called out excitedly, waving him over with a friendly grin. As Rodney approached, he felt the familiar butterflies of nerves fluttering in his stomach. This was his chance to get into the group and he knew he couldn't mess it up.

"Hey guys," Rodney greeted them, trying to sound casual. "What's the plan for tonight?"

"Party at McTagger's, he has this old barn outside of town," Matt replied as if it was common knowledge. "Should be a good time."

"First things first though," Jordan chimed in, eyeing the brown paper bag that Matt retrieved from his backpack. "Pre-drinks!"

"Snagged some alcohol from my family's liquor cabinet," Matt said proudly as he pulled out a bottle of vodka. The boys exchanged glances, excitement brewing beneath the surface.

"Alright, pass it around," Matt instructed, uncapping the bottle and taking a swig before handing it off to Steven. Rodney watched as the bottle made its way through the group, each boy gulping before passing it on.

When it reached Rodney, he hesitated. He had never drank alcohol before. Parker seemed to sense his hesitation, offering a gentle out. "You don't have to do it if you don't want to, man."

Matt scoffed, nudging Rodney playfully. "Come on, don't be a buzzkill. Just take a sip."

Seeking Matt's approval, Rodney swallowed his nerves and lifted the bottle to his lips. The vodka burned as it slid down his throat, and he choked back a cough as he handed the bottle to Parker.

"Nice one," Matt praised, grinning at Rodney's reddened face. "You'll fit right in tonight."

———-

The boys called a taxi and headed out to the barn. But as the evening wore on, the alcohol didn't quite sit well with Rodney. He felt his stomach churn, though he thought it might just be his nerves. He sent Derek a text, admitting he wasn't feeling well.

The response came quickly, full of concern: "Where are you? I can come get you."

The problem was that Rodney had no idea where they were. The barn, illuminated by strings of old Christmas lights, was packed with dancing bodies and pulsating music. As they entered the old barn, Matt split from the group. He pushed his way across the room to Ally, their hands entwined as they moved together, lost in each other's gaze.

Rodney couldn't tear his eyes away from the pair, both jealous and in awe of the seemingly happy couple. He felt drawn to Matt's confidence and charm, just as much as he longed for Ally's warmth and kindness. The conflicting emotions only added to his disorientation, leaving him unsteady on his feet.

"Seriously, where are you?" Derek's insistent text arrived, but Rodney still didn't have an answer.

"Lost," he replied, still struggling to keep his focus as he took a cup of spiked punch and began chugging, unaware of what it was. At this moment, all he wanted was someone to lean on – and perhaps, deep down, he wished anyone would look at him the way Matt and Ally looked at each other.

After chugging the whole cup, Rodney felt like he needed to sit down so he stumbled toward a row of fold-out chairs, telling himself that he would just sit for a minute. But the alcohol made his eyes feel heavy and he slipped into a dream. He found himself standing on the set of a dating game show, dazzling lights shining down on him. Parker, dressed in a glitzy suit, stepped up to the microphone. "And now, ladies and gentlemen, the moment you've all been waiting for! Rodney Thompson is about to make the most important decision of his life!"

"Choose! Choose!" chanted the imaginary audience, their voices pounding against his skull like a drum.

"Will it be our gorgeous and athletic Ally Matthews?" Parker asked, gesturing toward Ally, who stood poised in an elegant gown. She blew Rodney a kiss, her blue eyes sparkling like sapphires.

"Or will he choose our charming and confident Matt Jenkins?" Parker continued, as Matt appeared, dapper in a tailored suit, flashing a devastatingly alluring smile.

"Rodney," Parker said, his voice suddenly serious, "The choice is yours."

He hesitated, his mind torn between the two as his jealousy of Matt twisted into a form of adoration. The chant grew louder, pressing in on him from all sides. As indecision threatened to drown him, he jolted awake, and a wave of nausea surged through his body. Reality crashed back onto him, and he stumbled towards the barn doors, retching violently.

"Ugh, disgusting!" cried a party-goer, recoiling from the sight. Murmurs of disgust rippled through the crowd, sending a flush of shame across Rodney's face.

Unable to bear it any longer, he fled the party, desperate for fresh air and an escape from the judgemental eyes. His breath came in ragged gasps as he stumbled through the open field, the cold wind cutting through him like a knife.

"Rodney!" called a familiar voice, and he looked up to see Derek pulling up in his car. "Thank God, our generation posts everything on Instagram or I wouldn't have been able to find you. Get in – let's get you home."

"Thanks, Derek," Rodney mumbled, his voice hoarse from the ordeal. He climbed into the passenger seat, feeling a wave of relief wash over him as the warm air enveloped him.

"Drink lots of water when you get home," Derek advised, concern etching his features. "And listen, Rodney, don't try to be like those idiots. You're way more interesting than they will ever hope to be."

"Really?" Rodney asked, a small, hopeful smile playing on his lips.

"Absolutely," Derek replied, his voice soft and filled with sincerity. "Embrace your uniqueness, man."

"Thank you, Derek," Rodney whispered, touched by the older boy's kindness. As they pulled up to his house, he stepped out of the car, his heart lighter. "Would you want to hang out tomorrow?" Rodney took his chance at making a real friend.

Without hesitation, Derek responded "I'll see you tomorrow, buddy," With a final grateful nod, Rodney turned and headed inside, ready for the solace of his bed and the dreams that awaited him.

4

Or

Rodney wandered the fluorescent-lit aisles of Walmart, his eyes scanning each one for Ben and Jerry's ice cream. The store felt like an endless maze, and Rodney couldn't help but envision himself as an archaeologist navigating an ancient cavern. He darted around corners, avoiding employees as if they were mythological demons guarding the treasure he so desperately sought.

"Where is it?" he mumbled to himself, frustration bubbling inside him.

"Looking for something, young man?" A voice startled Rodney from behind, causing him to jump. The Walmart employee stood there eyeing him skeptically.

"Uh, yeah," stuttered Rodney, attempting to maintain his cool. "I'm just trying to find the ice cream aisle."

"Ah, the frozen aisle. Just take a left, then a right, and you'll be there," said the elderly woman, who flashed a smile before disappearing behind a massive skid of skin care cream.

"Thanks," Rodney replied to the now-empty space, feeling foolish.

He followed the directions and finally reached the frozen aisle. As he turned the corner, his heart skipped a beat. There, standing in front of the freezers, were Matt and Ally. They were laughing, their voices blending in a way that made Rodney's stomach churn. He had been avoiding Matt since the party, noting wanting to relive the night's events again. He still felt nauseous every time he thought about it.

"Come on, babe, you know I can't resist those caramel-filled drumsticks," Matt teased, playfully nudging Ally.

"Fine, I'll buy them for you but only if we watch Mean Girls. I can't believe you've never seen it," Ally countered, her blue eyes scanning the freezer for the drumsticks.

"Deal," Matt agreed, leaning in to steal a quick kiss.

"Ugh," thought Rodney, ducking behind the aisle to avoid detection. He hated seeing Ally kissing someone else, and he hated that he felt so jealous no matter how many times he told himself to stop feeling this way. He peered out cautiously, watching their interaction from a safe distance.

His mind drifted back to when he and Ally lived in Toronto before Matt was even part of the picture. They would make wizard-themed treats inspired by Harry Potter and watch the movies together. He wondered if Ally still remembered those times as fondly as he did. He really hadn't talked to her much the past week, she was always busy with Matt-related activities.

"Hey, Rodney!" Ally's voice snapped him back to reality. He hadn't realized they had spotted him.

"Uh, hey," he stammered, stepping into view.

"Didn't see you there," Matt said with a smirk, his arm draped around Ally's shoulders.

"Y-yeah, just looking for some ice cream," Rodney replied, trying to play it cool.

"Nice. Well, enjoy your ice cream, man," Matt said, giving Rodney a dismissive nod before attempting to lead Ally away, though she quickly rolled out from under his arm and turned back towards Rodney.

"Where'd you disappear to, I feel like I haven't seen you since the party. Did you see who threw up all over the barn?" Ally asked, her blue eyes sparkling like diamonds.

"Uh," Rodney hesitated, recalling his hasty exit from the chaotic gathering after getting sick. "I had to go home. My mom was looking for me." He scratched the back of his head nervously. "And I don't remember seeing anyone really, certainly no one throwing up."

Ally laughed, a laugh that sounded like wind chimes in the breeze. "That's okay, it was kind of a mess. We have to hang out again soon, alright?" She waved goodbye.

"Yeah, uh sure," Rodney agreed, but he knew she would be too busy to follow through with their plans. With that, the golden couple strolled away, leaving Rodney standing alone amidst the frozen goods.

Rodney stood there for a moment, having almost forgotten what he had come there for in the first place. He glanced at the freezer filled with Ben and Jerry's, but his appetite had vanished. With a heavy sigh, he turned and left the aisle empty-handed, the memory of Ally's laughter lingering in his ears.

———-

When Rodney arrived home, he tossed his jacket on the couch and flopped down beside it. A familiar buzz from his phone caught his attention – Derek was texting him.

"Hey, man, wanna go fishing?" Derek's message read, accompanied by a fishing pole emoji.

"Can't," Rodney typed back, lying through his thumbs. "Got some homework to do." The truth was, he just didn't have the energy to hang out with anyone, especially not after that awkward conversation with Ally and Matt.

"Alright, no worries. Hit me up if you change your mind!" Derek replied.

Rodney sighed, sinking deeper into the couch cushions. He tried to focus on the television, but his thoughts kept drifting back to Ally and Matt, their laughter haunting him like a cruel joke the world was playing on him. Did Ally not notice that he had been texting her to hang out almost every day, and she always had an excuse locked and loaded? Rodney decided some video games might be needed to pull him out of his funk. He hoped Zain would be online to play with him.

Rodney made his way across the hall and to his room. His fingers hovered over his keyboard as he took his usual seat at his desk. He took a deep breath and clicked "Join" – Phasmaphobia was his escape today. The game loaded, and he found himself in a virtual haunted house alongside three random other players, Zain wasn't online today. Scrolling through their usernames, one caught his eye: StrathVegasPark. He had seen Parker use it as his password before in the computer lab, could it be?

"Hey, Parker?" Rodney hesitated, speaking into his headset. "Is that you?"

"Rodney? No way!" Parker's familiar voice rang out, he could hear Parker adjusting his headset as if it almost fell off his head. "What are the odds, right?"

"Pretty crazy," Rodney agreed, a small smile spreading across his face. Parker seemed like someone he could actually be friends with. As they navigated the spooky corridors, he couldn't help but get lost in Parker's laugh, whenever he fled the building at the slightest noise. It almost made him forget about his awkward encounter with Matt and Ally.

"By the way," Parker said, his tone turning more serious, as they started their second mission "How are you holding up after the party?"

"Uh, I'm okay," Rodney lied, focusing intently on taking an EKG reading. "Why do you ask?"

"I should've stopped you from drinking so much," Parker admitted, Rodney could his face turn red as he realized Parker knew what he had done at the party. "Matt can be pretty pushy, you know? Like, he doesn't always realize when he's gone too far. Honestly, I should have told him to back off,"

"It's OK, Parker," Rodney sighed, feeling embarrassed about the whole thing. He fiddled with the edge of his hoodie, feeling vulnerable as he added, "I mean I don't know why I did it, I guess Matt has this weirdly magnetic vibe, it's like I want him to like me. I just... can't really explain why, you know? And..." His words trailed off, but the truth slipped out anyway. "Ally is dating him so there has to be something there, she is so amazing and if she sees something in him then it has to be there."

"Hold up," Parker sounded confused over the headset. Rodney could hear him shift in his chair. "Just the way you talk about Ally, you two are just friends, right? Like you aren't thinking about her romantically... because Matt would kill you if he thought you were trying to be his friend just so you could steal her from him."

It took a moment for Rodney to process how to get out of this one, the gears slowly turning in his head. Rodney's heart raced, realizing he might have said too much. The more he thought about it, the more obvious it was. Rodney's silence had gone on for way too long.

"Look," Parker began, his cheery tone from earlier completely gone, "going after someone else's girlfriend is wrong, no matter how douchey the guy might be. I know you and Ally have a history, but you can't pretend to be someone's friend just to get their girl. I mean is she the only reason you hung out with us?"

"Of course not!" Rodney protested, feeling a little dizzy. "Parker, I see you as my friend. I never meant to—"

"Whatever." And with that, StrathVegasPark left the game.

Rodney stared at the space where Parker's character had been, feeling the weight of his own words suffocating him. He didn't even notice the ghost approaching him from behind until his character dropped to the floor dead. All Rodney could think was, what if Parker told Matt everything? What if Ally found out about it? As negative scenarios began to pour into his mind, Rodney felt like he was drowning.

His fingers hovered above his phone screen, hesitating before finally typing out a message to Derek. "Hey, I've had the worst day ever. Can we talk?" He hit send and stared at the glowing screen, praying Derek would answer the text.

Within minutes, a knock at the door startled Rodney as he sat alone in his room. He opened it to find Derek standing there, grinning broadly, holding two fishing poles. "Thought talking in person might be the better way to go on this one," Derek said, his eyes crinkling in the corners as he smiled. "Come on, let's go fishing."

"Uh, sure," Rodney agreed, still feeling a bit dazed, Derek had actually rushed to his side when he needed him. They walked together towards the Sydenham River in silence, the sun casting golden rays through the trees as it began to set. Once they reached the water, Derek handed Rodney a fishing pole, and they cast their lines into the calm current.

"Derek," Rodney started, his voice barely audible over the gentle lapping of the water. "I think I messed up with Parker. I kind of hinted I want to be more than friends with Ally. I know he is friends with Matt but we were having such a good time, I let my guard down. What if he tells Matt everything, He'll kill me. Parker seemed kind of pissed at me about it."

"Ah, I wouldn't worry too much about that one, we all make mistakes," Derek exhaled slowly, nodding in understanding. "It must have been hard for Parker to hear that."

"What do you mean?" Rodney asked, wondering why it would be so hard for Parker to find out he liked Ally.

"Well I mean Parker sits next to you in every class you have together, or at least that is what you have told me. He is your friend, but he is also Matt's. I think he probably feels very conflicted right now about what to do." Derek reasoned.

"Maybe I shouldn't have said anything. I just feel like he is someone I could tell anything to. You know, like you," Rodney's gaze wandered towards his bobber as it drifted on the river's surface.

"Look, man," Derek said, as he set his hook. "Parker's a good guy. He'll forgive your slip up, but you're gonna have to put in the work to show him you're really not just there to take Ally away from Matt."

"Thanks, Derek," Rodney replied, watching him bring in his catch, a small sunfish. "You're a true friend."

"Anytime, buddy." Derek flashed him another warm smile before returning the tiny fish to the river.

———-

Later that night, Rodney laid in bed, staring at his phone. He took a deep breath and typed out a message to Parker. "I'm really sorry for what I said earlier. Yes, I had feelings for Ally but I don't think they are romantic feelings, I think I might just be missing the time I used to spend with my BFF. I feel like she just doesn't have time to hang out with me like we used to. It's kind of been driving me crazy lately, but I don't want to lose you as a friend over this." He hesitated a moment before hitting send, the message he had spent hours thinking about didn't seem as great as it did in his head. Reading it over he knew it sounded kind of desperate but he really didn't know what else to do.

As he set his phone down on the nightstand, preparing himself for a sleepless night filled with worry, he hoped he would find a text from Parker in the morning.

———-

The morning sunlight filtered through the tall windows lining the high school hallway, Rodney and Ally stood discussing their latest geography assignment. Rodney's brow furrowed in concentration, his fingers tapping nervously on the cover of his textbook.

"Ally, do you think silicon or aluminum is the primary resource used in computer hard drives? I'm leaning towards silicon, but this textbook is older than computers," he said, his voice lighting up at his own joke.

"Silicon does seem more likely," Ally agreed, but she seemed kind of distant from the project. "But maybe we could look up some more information during lunch on the internet, it might actually be from this century."

Their conversation was abruptly interrupted as Matt pushed his way between them, his muscular frame easily dwarfing Rodney's slight build. "Hey babe, come watch me practice in the gym. I've been working on my layups."

"Um, Matt, Ally and I have this project to work on," Rodney stammered, clutching his textbook tighter.

"Relax, man. It can wait. Ally told me it wasn't due till Thursday," Matt replied dismissively, his dark eyes focused solely on Ally. "Come on, Ally Cat."

"Yeah, we can finish it up later," Ally conceded, giving Rodney an apologetic smile before following Matt down the hallway, leaving Rodney feeling abandoned yet again by the person he called his best friend.

As Rodney leaned against the cold metal of a nearby locker, his thoughts raced. Why did Matt always have to steal Ally away like that? He felt a sudden pang of jealousy, quickly followed by a wave of guilt for his feelings towards his friend when she was with someone else.

"Rodney," a familiar voice called out. Parker approached, his messy curls bouncing with each step, and his glasses perched precariously on his nose. "About the other night… I wanted to apologize for my outburst during our game. I get the feeling of losing a friend, and it sucks. I would be happy to talk about it with you if you want?"

Rodney's heart skipped a beat, overjoyed that Parker understood the feelings he had been having. "Thank you, it was hard enough moving here and thinking I would never see her again, now she is here too and I still never see her," he replied, gazing down the hallway where Ally had just been. "And I'm sorry too, for what I said. I didn't mean to make you feel like I was just hanging around you guys because I wanted to be with Ally. Honestly, I like hanging out with you a lot."

"Thanks, Rodney. I feel the same way, I mean, Matt hasn't exactly wanted to hit the courts like we used to since he started dating Ally," Parker admitted, an awkward smile tugging at the corners of his lips. "Maybe we can fill that friendship void with each other,"

"Definitely," Rodney agreed, relief washing over him like a cool breeze on a hot day. "want to head to class together?"

"Sure thing," As they walked toward the classroom together, Rodney felt excited about having another friend in town.

5

Maybe

The afternoon sun shone brightly through the cafeteria's high windows, as students sat and ate what the school called lunch. Rodney absent-mindedly picked at his turkey wrap, his thoughts occupied by Ally and Matt's latest post. Beside him, Derek took a bite of his pizza, chewing slower than normal as he took Rodney's saddened expression.

"Alright, man," Derek finally said, wiping his hands on a napkin. "I think it's time for plan B. We need to find a way to get you more popularity, you know so you get to Ally's level." He leaned back in the blue plastic chair, the wheels turning in his head. "What if you threw a massive party? It could really help you get your name out there."

Rodney looked up at Derek, the fear clear in his eyes. "A party?" He hesitated before admitting, "I don't know. My mom is strictly against all things fun, and I have never hosted a party. What if something goes wrong?"

"Come on man, we're teens, making bad choices is our whole deal," Derek reasoned "I'm sure she would forgive one party, and if you did it while she wasn't there, she wouldn't even know. We could have the place cleaned up before she even got there."

"Well, my mom and sister will be gone Saturday night, so I guess I could do it then." Rodney let slip as he thought Derek's words over.

"Great!" Derek exclaimed, slapping Rodney on the back.

Rodney almost choked on his sandwich from the hit. "But I've still never thrown a party before, Derek. What if no one shows up?" Rodney coughed as he reached for his water.

"Trust me, buddy," Derek reassured him with a wicked grin. "You throw a killer party, and everyone will be talking about it Monday morning, and suddenly every popular kid wants you at theirs. Just make sure to post about it on Instagram and TikTok so people know it's happening."

The bell rang signalling the end of lunch, Rodney couldn't shake the growing feeling that he was going to be sick. The idea of hosting a party both thrilled and terrified him. People will come to my party, he thought, and mom will never find out. With every step down the crowded hallways, no matter how much he tried to convince himself otherwise, he felt like the part would fail.

———-

After school, Rodney hesitantly posted about the party on Instagram and TikTok, his fingers trembling as he hit 'post'. He anxiously refreshed the pages, hoping for a flood of RSVPs, but as the minutes ticked by and no responses came in, his worry only intensified. He imagined himself standing alone in his living room, surrounded by streamers and snacks, the music echoing through the empty house.

"Hey, it'll be fine," Derek assured him before heading out to his bus. "Just give people some time to get home and read it. They'll start RSVPing soon, I promise."

Rodney dragged his feet as he walked toward the front of the school, his mind a whirlwind of thoughts about the impending party. He passed by a group of girls giggling over their phones, and he couldn't help but notice Ally in the centre of it all, her laughter as bright as the sun. She was always saying they should hang out more, so surely she'd come to his party.

"Hey, Ally," he called out, mustering every ounce of courage in his body. She turned to him with her signature Ally smile.

"Hi, Rodney! What's up?" she asked, seeing the concerning expression on Rodney's face.

"Uh, I'm having a party this Saturday night, and I was hoping you could come," he stammered, trying to sound casual but feeling anything but.

Ally's face fell ever so slightly, and she shifted her weight from one foot to another. "Oh, Rodney, I don't think I can make it. Matt has to work that night, and I'd feel weird going to a party without him." Her words struck him like a dagger, and his heart sank.

"Ah, that's cool," he lied, forcing a smile onto his face. "No worries!" his face wobbling as he tried not to cry. Why did Ally need Matt with her to go to his party?

As Ally returned to her friends, Rodney shook off the sting of rejection and continued. A thought dawned on him, Parker, he fumbled to pull his phone from his pocket. If anyone could lift his spirits, it was Parker.

"Hey, man," Rodney said when Parker picked up. "I'm throwing a party this Saturday, and I was hoping you could come."

Parker paused for a moment before answering. "I'd love to, Rodney, but my family has movie night every Saturday. It's kind of mandatory," he explained, a hint of disappointment in his voice.

"Right, I understand," Rodney said, trying to hide the panic that was creeping up on him. He was starting to feel as though his party would be straight out of a comedy, with the frat house overrun by nerds while the cool kids remained conspicuously absent.

"Thanks anyway," he added, forcing himself out of the terrible vision. "I hope you can make it next time."

"Definitely," Parker promised, his voice sounded sincere and warm.

Rodney saw his mom parked in the lot waiting, his heart heavy with worry. If his own friends couldn't make it to his party, who would? He climbed into the car, anxious his party was a failure before it even began.

———-

When the night of the party had finally arrived, Rodney paced nervously across the beige living room carpet. He couldn't help but cast a critical eye over the scattered dollar store Halloween decorations that adorned the walls, a few plastic bats, ghost streamers, and one terribly carved Jack-o'-lantern. He sighed, checking his phone again and rereading Derek's text: "Sorry dude, gotta take my sister to hockey. I'll be there later."

"Great," he muttered under his breath, tossing the phone aside. It was as if all his worst fears were coming true. No one he knew had said yes, he was about to play host to ten total strangers, with no one there to ease him into it. He could almost feel the panic attack taking hold.

Just as these thoughts threatened to consume him, there came a knock on the door. His heart leaped into his throat, and he quickly scrambled to start the music before rushing to answer it.

"Hey, um, welcome!" he stammered as he opened the door to an unfamiliar couple decked out in Halloween attire. They looked cool and nonchalant, barely acknowledging him before slipping inside. Rodney blinked, slightly confused but grateful anyone had shown up at all. Madison followed close behind them, her eyes taking in the sad state of the party with an air of disapproval.

"Nice place, Rodney. Didn't this party start, like an hour ago?" she said flatly, her tone betraying her lack of enthusiasm.

"Um yeah, but there is…. I mean some people are just running late," he replied, forcing a smile. Inside, he cringed at her reaction, wondering if this whole thing had been a mistake.

As the couple settled onto the couch and began making out, Madison occupied herself with her phone, leaving Rodney alone in the sea of inadequacy that was his party. With only three guests, he couldn't shake the feeling that this would go down as the lamest Halloween party in history.

"Maybe a masked killer will burst through the door and end it all right now," he thought, staring at the door as if willing it to happen.

But instead of a killer, there came another knock at the door. Rodney wasn't sure he wanted anyone else to see this disaster of a party, but with a huff, he made his way over to the door. He opened it… and there she was, dressed as Sydney Prescott from the Scream movies. Ally smiled and waved when she saw Rodney, her eyes sparkling with excitement. Rodney couldn't believe it, she came, she was really at the party.

"Hey, Rodney!" she called out, making her way over to him.

"Ally! You came!" he blurted out, surprise and relief flooding through him.

"Yeah," she replied with a grin. "I figured I had to see your first-ever party."

Rodney's heart swelled with gratitude, his earlier fears momentarily forgotten. If Ally was here, then nothing else really mattered to him.

"I thought you couldn't come because Matt was busy?" Rodney said as they stood amid the party's lacklustre atmosphere.

"Well, I thought about it, and I realized supporting my friends should come first," Ally replied with a warm smile. "Besides, I can have fun without Matt,"

Rodney looked around at the meagre decorations and sparse crowd, feeling a wave of embarrassment wash over him. "I'm sorry this is so… lame."

"Hey, it's not that bad," Ally said optimistically. "And besides, I think I know what to do." She whipped out her phone and tapped away at the screen for a moment. Within minutes, the doorbell rang again and the entire yoga club, dressed in a variety of creative costumes, flooded into the living room. Laughter and chatter filled the air, and Rodney couldn't believe how quickly the party was transformed.

"Nice job, Ally," he said appreciatively, watching as his once-empty house came alive with energy.

"Teamwork makes the dream work!" she joked, giving him a playful nudge.

Just then, Derek burst through the door with a group of grade 11s in tow, adding even more life to the party. He made his way over to Rodney, hugging him.

"Sorry I'm late, dude," Derek apologized. "Had to make a pickup before I came over here."

"Better late than never," Rodney replied, grateful for his friend's support. Derek nodded, then gestured toward a girl named Sky, leaving Rodney to mingle with her. As the night wore on, Rodney talked to Ally about their shared love for horror movies.

"Nothing beats the classics like Friday the 13th, Halloween, and A Nightmare on Elm Street," Rodney enthused, watching Ally's eyes light up as they talked.

"OMG, right!" she exclaimed. "I could watch those movies on a loop."

Ally's phone buzzed with an incoming text. Glancing down, she saw it was from Matt, saying he was free now and that she should come over. A moment of hesitation crossed her face before she decided to ignore the message.

"Anyway," she said, redirecting her attention back to Rodney and their conversation, "did we ever see the original Texas Chainsaw Massacre together?"

"Ugh no, I think that one is too bloody with no plot" Rodney admitted.

"That is what makes it scary! I miss watching horror movies," Ally lamented, "Matt hates them so we don't watch them."

"Maybe we can have a horror movie night," Rodney suggested, giving her a slight smile, "So you can catch up on what you missed."

"I would like that," Ally said, smiling to herself. Everyone else seemed to fade into the background as their conversation continued.

———-

As the night drew to a close, guests began to filter out one by one. Rodney couldn't help but feel proud as they left, realizing that despite his initial reservations, he had successfully thrown his first party.

"Hey," Ally said, sliding up next to him once the last guest had disappeared through the front door. "That was really fun, Rodney. Let's set a date for that horror movie night soon, OK?"

Rodney's heart did a little somersault at her words. "Yeah, definitely. Maybe next week if you're free?"

"I'll check and text you when I get home. Goodnight, Rodney," she said warmly, squeezing his arm before heading home herself.

"Goodnight, Ally," he called after her, watching her retreating figure until she vanished into the darkness.

With a sigh of satisfaction, Rodney turned his attention to the mess that now littered his living room. As he picked up discarded cups and plates, he couldn't help but replay the night's events in his head, savouring each moment spent with Ally.

A knock on the door pulled him from his memories, he looked at it in confusion. Approaching it cautiously he swung it open, revealing Parker standing there sheepishly, a bag of McDonald's clutched in his hands.

"Hey, man." Parker rubbed the back of his neck, his cheeks tinged pink with embarrassment. "I'm sorry I missed the party because the whole family night thing. I brought Big Macs as an apology?"

"Come on in," Rodney said, grinning and stepping aside to let Parker enter. "Better late than never, right?"

"Thanks," Parker replied, relief evident in his voice as he followed Rodney to the living room. They settled onto the couch, unwrapping their burgers as Rodney started *IT: Chapter One* on the TV.

"Nothing like horror movies and fast food to end the night," Parker joked, taking a big bite of his Big Mac.

"Agreed," Rodney laughed, he was overjoyed Parker had shown up at all. They settled into a comfortable silence, stealing the odd glance at each other as they watched Pennywise terrorize the Losers Club.

As Parker cracked jokes about the dancing clown, Rodney was struck by a sudden realization: this was easy, why couldn't hanging out with Ally be this easy?

6

It's

Rodney sat uncomfortably on the cold metal bench at the Strathroy Middlesex arena, shivering slightly from the chill in the air. His breath formed a small cloud as he exhaled, staring down at his phone screen. The time read 6:30 pm, making him frown in confusion. He scrolled back through his texts, searching for the one from Ally who had told him to meet her there at 6 pm sharp.

"Where is she?" he wondered out loud, his voice barely audible over the chatter and laughter of the families gliding around the rink. Trying to calm his nerves he decided to do a few laps around the rink before the Free Skate event was over.

As Rodney got off the bench, he clumsily bumped into Parker, who was skating nearby, a plaid knitted scarf slung over his shoulder. They both seemed equally surprised to see each other.

"Hey, Parker," Rodney stammered, trying to recover from the unexpected encounter. "I'm so sorry, I didn't see you there,"

Parker shook his head, pushing his glasses up the bridge of his nose. "It's fine, I didn't exactly try to swerve out of the way. Guess I was just lost in thought, you know? Everything just flows when I'm in motion."

"Ah, I get it," Rodney replied. "Do you mind if I skate around with you?"

"Not at all," Parker said with a smile.

The two boys glided around the ice, enjoying the quiet companionship that came with not needing to fill the silence with words. As they skated, Rodney couldn't help but think about Ally's absence, and his mind conjured up an elaborate fantasy. In it, Ally was trapped in a tower guarded by a fearsome dragon, and Rodney donned a suit of golden armour to storm the castle and rescue her. The horrifying dragon prepared to blast Rodney with flames as he charged the massive beast, sword drawn.

The loud, jarring clang of the bell announcing the end of Free Skate snapped Rodney back to reality. Parker looked amused, skating a little closer to him.

"Where do you go when you zone out like that? You looked like you were a million miles away," Parker teased.

Rodney laughed it off, feeling his cheeks grow warm in embarrassment. "Maybe one day I'll let you in on my secret daydreams."

"Deal," Parker grinned, before hesitating for a moment. "Hey, there's a cultural food festival happening this weekend. Do you want to go?"

"Sure, sounds fun," Rodney replied, trying not to sound too eager. "Who else is coming?"

Parker scratched the back of his neck, looking almost shy. "Actually, I was thinking it would just be the two of us. I'd really like to get to know you better, Rodney."

At that moment, Rodney felt an unfamiliar warmth bloom in his chest and the warmth returned to his cheeks. It almost felt like Parker was asking him out, and he couldn't explain why a small part of him hoped that was the case. He stammered out a response, as he tried to convince himself he was thinking too much into it. "Yeah, yeah, I'll see you there."

As Rodney skated away from Parker, his thoughts raced, trying to make sense of these strange feelings he was having.

———-

The next day, Rodney slouched at the library desk, fiddling with the corners of his notebook as he thought about what some would wear to a cultural food festival. Was the food festival a date? Did he want it to be a date? His stomach churned in knots as asked himself why he would even think it was a date.

"Hey, Rodney," Derek said, sliding into the seat next to him. "You look like you're going to be sick, buddy. What's up?"

"Ally stood me up last night at the arena," Rodney blurted out, his voice cracking slightly. He chewed on his bottom lip, unsure if he wanted to share more.

"Ouch," Derek winced. "That's rough, man." He paused for a moment, studying Rodney's face before offering some advice. "Maybe, it's time you tried dating someone else? I'm not saying give up on Ally, just suggesting you see what else is out there. Plus, it could make Ally jealous, which would make her realize she has feelings for you."

Rodney considered Derek's words but couldn't see himself dating anyone right now, even as Parker's face entered his mind. "Yeah, maybe you're right," he conceded, forcing the intrusive thoughts from his head.

"Trust me, Rodney," Derek said with a knowing grin. "Go talk to Madison. She's practically a matchmaker. She'll find you a date and in no time at all, Ally will realize what she is missing out on."

———-

After school, Rodney spotted Madison walking home, her brown hair bouncing with each step. As he approached, she looked up and smiled. "Hey, Rodney."

"Oh, uh hey," he replied, surprised she even knew his name. "I heard you're kind of a… matchmaker?" He scratched his head awkwardly. "I'm looking to … um … maybe try dating."

Madison raised an eyebrow, clearly flattered. "Well, I might be able to help, but I'll need to know like, everything about you. You know, to figure out who you are before I recommend someone."

"Uh, sure," Rodney agreed, feeling a little uneasy, "Do I take some kind of matching-making quiz or something?"

"LOL, Rodney that is too cute," Madison laughed, "No I need to see what you are really like you know. I'll just shadow you for a bit, you won't even know I'm there."

"Oh… Uh OK if that is how it works," Rodney could feel his heart start to race at the idea of being watched by someone he hardly knew.

"Great, now give me your phone." Rodney handed her his phone and she quickly typed her number into his contacts. "Text me and we'll be in touch."

As Rodney walked away, he couldn't shake the feeling of unease that settled in his stomach at the thought of someone assessing his every move. He pulled out his phone and typed a quick message to Madison, saying he'd changed his mind. He pocketed his phone and breathed a small sigh of relief.

———-

A few days later, Rodney found himself standing at the entrance of Victoria Park. The lively chatter of people exploring the different booths and playing games filled the air, accompanied by the enticing aromas of various cuisines wafting through the park. He glanced around nervously, searching for any sign of Parker.

"Hey, Rodney!" Parker waved from a short distance away, his curly hair bouncing as he jogged over. He was dressed in blue jeans and a buffalo plaid button-up that seemed to make him even more endearing in Rodney's eyes. But just as quickly as the thought entered his mind, Rodney shook it off, determined not to let these confusing emotions he'd been having get the better of him.

"Hey, thanks for inviting me," Rodney said, trying to sound casual. "So, where do you want to start?"

Parker flashed a warm smile. "Let's check out the food trucks. I'm starving."

As they wove their way through the bustling crowd, Rodney couldn't help but steal glances at Parker as he led the way. Finally, they ended up in line for a Thai-Mexican fusion truck called The Thai Volcano.

"Two orders of pad thai tacos, please," Parker said, turning to Rodney with a grin. "It's on me."

"Are you sure?" Rodney hesitated, feeling a sudden rush of warmth in his cheeks. Parker was being really nice to him and Rodney couldn't help but feel like it was in a more than just friends kind of way.

"Absolutely," Parker replied, handing over some cash to the vendor.

They found a bench to sit on and began eating their oddly delicious tacos under the shade of a large maple tree.

"So, Mr. Fitz has me sweating about this upcoming math test," Parker started as he picked up his first taco, trying to figure out his plan of attack.

"Mr. Fitz?" Rodney tried to think about all the teachers he had met at the school, he could count them all on his fingers. "Wait is he the one who acts like a squirrel sometimes?" Rodney silently thanked Derek for telling him about the odd teacher earlier.

"The one and the same," Parker laughed.

"Seriously, what's up with that guy?" Rodney chuckled, taking a bite of his taco.

"Who knows? Maybe he's part squirrel," Parker joked, causing Rodney to laugh and almost choke. "Be right back! Just have to hit the washroom."

Parker disappeared into the crowd leaving Rodney's thoughts to wander. He imagined leaning in and kissing Parker, feeling his soft lips against his own, their hands entwined. The vividness of the fantasy took him by surprise, leaving him both excited and terrified. Was it normal to feel this way about another guy?

His phone buzzed and he dove for it, desperate to stop thinking about Parker this way. A text from Madison appeared on the screen: "You were supposed to text me! Lucky for you I was able to track down your number. I have a friend here. She totally wants to meet you ASAP."

Rodney paused, he thought he did text Madison, but taking a look through his texts he discovered the numbers were different. Then it hit him, a girl was interested in him. He looked back toward the bathrooms and saw no sign of Parker. His thoughts spiralled, dating a girl was normal, and every movie he saw told him so. He didn't know why he was feeling the way he felt about Parker and honestly, he didn't want to put any more thought into it.

"Sorry, Parker," he muttered under his breath, quickly finishing his tacos and leaving the park. He knew what he was doing was wrong but he just wanted to get out of there. He sent Parker a quick text about feeling sick as he fled the park.

———-

The school bus came to a halt, and Rodney stepped off, his backpack heavy with textbooks. He took a deep breath, hoping for a fresh start to the week.

"Rodney!" The familiar voice of Parker cut through the air like a knife, causing Rodney to freeze in place. As he turned around, he saw Parker storming towards him, his eyes filled with anger.

"Hey, Parker," Rodney said cautiously, trying to keep his voice steady. "What's up?"

"Where were you?" Parker demanded, pointing an accusing finger at him. "I went to your house to see how you were doing and your mom said you weren't there. Did you lie to me about being sick!"

"Uh, I… I just walked over to the convenience store for some meds, is all," Rodney stammered, his face flushing with embarrassment. He didn't want to admit that he'd left because he was having confusing feelings for him.

"You expect me to believe that?" Parker snapped, staring at Rodney with a hurt expression. "You know what? Forget it. Come talk to me when you are ready to tell me the truth."

Before Rodney could say anything, Parker turned on his heel and stormed away, leaving Rodney standing there, feeling like he'd just been punched in the gut. Guilt twisted inside him, and he swallowed hard, fighting back tears.

"Rodney, are you okay?" Ally's soft voice came from behind him. She seemed genuinely concerned and he turned to meet to see her, her blue eyes wide with worry.

"Ally," Rodney forced a weak smile, trying to brush off the encounter with Parker. "Yeah, I'm fine. Sorry if you heard any of that,"

"Yeah…. Sorry, I've been so flakey lately," Ally said apologetically. "Matt's been going through some stuff, and he really needed me. What happened between you and Parker?"

"Um, we're fighting over a girl," Rodney lied, not wanting Ally to ask too many questions. He knew Ally wouldn't judge him, but he wasn't sure himself about how he felt.

"Really?" Ally raised an eyebrow in surprise. "I didn't know you were interested in anyone."

As if on cue, Erica appeared, her dark hair pulled back in a messy bun. "Hey, Rodney," she greeted him with a smile. "Would you walk me to class?"

"Sure," Rodney agreed, torn between relief and regret. "Ally, I'll tell you more later, okay?"

"Okay," Ally said, watching as Rodney and Erica walked away together. A pang of jealousy crept its way through her chest, and she found herself wanting to be the one walking beside him. She couldn't help but miss the conversations they used to have on the way to class in middle school. With a deep breath, she pushed the thought away, chiding herself for letting her imagination get the best of her. Shaking her head, she turned her attention to Matt, who stood waiting for her a few feet away.

"Let's go, Ally Cat," he said, a hint of concern in his voice. "We don't want to be late for class." She nodded, forcing a smile onto her face, and hurried to join him, trying to ignore the lingering image of Rodney and Erica walking away hand in hand.

7

Parker,

Ally leaned against her open locker, half-listening to Luke as he animatedly described their latest science project. "So, we're creating a portrait of a family using a genetic grid," he explained, gesturing enthusiastically with his hands. "All three of my kids got green hair, is that even possible?" Matt and Parker nodded along while trying not to laugh at the drawing he made of his pretend family.

"Sounds pretty cool," Ally chimed in, her gaze drifting down the crowded hallway. She spotted Rodney walking alongside Erica, deep in conversation. And she couldn't take her eyes off them, no matter how many times she told herself to. "Looks like Rodney and Erica are still going strong. He doesn't seem to have time for anyone else anymore." She muttered not noticing that Parker's eyes had also drifted in Rodney's direction.

Matt scoffed. "Does it even matter? The guy's been acting weird since he got here, and now he's with the weird girl. If you ask me it is a match made in heaven." His tone was dismissive, and he couldn't help but feel annoyed by the attention Ally was wasting on them.

"Rodney was my best friend before I moved here, Matt. His friendship means the world to me," she snapped, her blue eyes flashing with anger. Without another word, she slammed her locker shut and stormed off, leaving her friends behind. Matt hesitated for a moment before following her, calling out apologies as he tried to catch up.

As Parker and Luke watched the scene unfold, a question struck Parker. Where had he seen this before? Was it just him or was Ally acting like Rodney did whenever he saw her with Matt?

———-

After science class, Parker caught up with Ally near the exit. "Hey, can we talk?" he asked, his voice strained. Ally frowned, curious about his sudden seriousness. She nodded, folding her arms across her chest.

"Look, um are you jealous that Rodney is with someone else?" Parker blurted out, his glasses sliding down his nose as he spoke. Ally's face flushed a deep crimson, but Parker didn't seem to notice as he pressed on. " I mean you practically ignored Rodney this whole since you started dating Matt, standing him up and things. But now that he's got a girlfriend, suddenly you act like all you want to do is hang with your apparent best friend."

Parker paused for a breath, his brown eyes locked on Ally's shocked expression. "Rodney had a huge crush on you at the beginning of the year, anyone with eyes could see that. You don't know what it's like to like someone who doesn't like you back, Ally, and it's not fair to keep Rodney around as a backup plan." His voice cracked, and he turned away from her, blinking back tears.

Ally stood there, dumbfounded by Parker's outburst. Her mind raced, was Parker right? She opened her mouth to speak, but no words came out. Before she could find the right thing to say, Parker rushed off, leaving her alone with her thoughts and a newfound realization: she might have feelings for Rodney, which could be the weird feeling she gets seeing him with someone else.

———-

Throughout the day, Ally found herself lost in thought, her fingers idly tapping against the edge of her desk as she stared out the classroom window. The tiny snow crystals danced whimsically in the breeze, she wished she could be free like them. She wished she didn't have to think about what Parker said but the words stuck to the back of her mind like they were placed there with superglue.

Ignoring the constant buzzing of her phone, she pondered whether she had truly led Rodney on. When she had first met him, there was a part of her that was drawn to his quiet sensitivity, and she had imagined they might end up together in grade 6 when they spent every moment after school together writing a Doctor Who fanfic. She loved his creativity and how he smiled every time she came up with a great idea. But then everything happened with his dad, Rodney retreated into his shell, unlike Matt who boldly pursued her the moment she arrived at SDCI. But Ally couldn't help but hang on to the way Rodney had made her feel back then.

Finally, the bell rang, releasing her from her self-imposed prison. She collected her things and hurried home, eager for the solace of her bedroom.

"Ugh," Ally groaned as she tossed her bag onto the bench at the front entrance, her head pounding as her mind tried to get her to pick between Matt and Rodney. Desperate for relief, she made some tea with honey, for some reason tea always seemed to calm her down. As she sipped her comforting drink, Mark, her brother, entered the kitchen.

"Hey. What's wrong with you?" he asked, concern etched in the creases of his forehead.

Ally hesitated, "Have you ever thought something was one way but really it was another, and now that you realize that, you wonder if you made a wrong decision? But if you try to fix it you may also end up hurting someone so really you feel trapped in a game you can't win?"

"Um, is there like a dictionary for translating Ally to a regular human?" Mark half-joked, "You are going to need to give me a little more here,"

Ally sighed "Turns out Rodney liked me, or likes me, I don't know. Well, I kind of knew he liked me but with everything that happened with his dad, he just wasn't the same Rodney." She stirred her tea, watching the ripples flow through the warm liquid.

"Oh, so that is why he hasn't been around here much since we moved," Mark said taking a seat next to her.

"Yeah.. the thing is, a part of me chose Matt so I would stop romantically thinking of Rodney. I guess that is why I have been avoiding Rodney since we moved here too, I could tell he was into me but I wasn't into him, well I mean this version of him. Am I a bad person? What do I do?" She looked at Mark as if he was hiding the answer somewhere on himself.

"That is a tough one. Honestly, a first for me, but Ally you have to be you. Trust yourself to make the choices." Mark offered, still unsure of the whole situation.

Ally nodded but wished Mark could have just given her a clear answer. She hugged Mark tightly, grateful for his support. "Thanks, Mark."

"Anytime," he said, squeezing her back.

———-

The next morning, Ally walked briskly towards the school entrance as the sun rose in the sky. She clutched her backpack straps tightly, prepared for the conversations she knew she had to have.

"Hey, Parker," Ally said, catching up with him just outside the school doors. His messy curls danced in the breeze as he turned to face her.

"Ally," he replied cautiously. "What's up?"

"Look, I wanted to talk to you about yesterday," she began, fiddling with her backpack straps. "You were right. I do… or did have feelings for Rodney, and I wasn't being fair to him, or myself. And you are a true friend for pointing that out to me, I was acting crazy."

Parker studied her for a moment, his eyes searching hers before nodding slowly. "I appreciate you admitting that, Ally. And I am sorry too, I definitely could have gone about it differently."

"You did what you had to do," she replied, a relieved smile stretching across her face. "And I promise I'll try to be more decisive from now on, and let people know how I really feel."

"Sounds like a good plan," Parker said, offering her a small smile. "Still friends?"

"Still friends," Ally breathed, allowing herself a brief moment to revel in the mending of their friendship before turning her thoughts to the next difficult conversation she needed to have.

———-

As the final bell rang, Ally's pulse quickened, her palms damp and sweaty. She stood near the lockers, scanning the sea of students for Rodney's familiar face. At last, she spotted him, his slight build emerging from the throng, his short brown hair ruffled from the long day.

"Rodney," she called out, her voice wavering slightly. He looked up, surprise registering on his features as she approached.

"Hey, Ally," he said warily, his eyes darting around as if searching for an escape route. "What's up?"

"Can we talk?" she asked, her voice barely more than a whisper.

"Uh, sure," he replied hesitantly, entering his locker combination.

"Listen," Ally began, taking a deep breath before she began. "I need to be honest with you. I… I did have feelings for you when we were back in Toronto. And I am sorry that I have been avoiding you."

Rodney blinked, his eyes widening in shock. He opened his mouth to speak, but she pressed on before he could find the words.

"The real reason I skipped out on skating with you," she continued, her voice shaking, "is because I felt like it would be cheating on Matt because a part of me still wants to be with you, but I have to let it go. So we can both be happy."

For a moment, Rodney stood motionless, as if he were standing in front of an oncoming bus that threatened to topple him over. Finally, he found his voice, though it came out as more of a whisper. "Ally, I…"

"Look," she interrupted, blinking back tears, "I just wanted to say I'm sorry, but I still want to be friends. I have really missed my best friend, I don't think I realized it until now."

Without waiting for a response, Ally turned and walked away, leaving Rodney standing there, alone and speechless, still unsure about what just happened.

"Hey, man!" Derek's voice cut through the fog, snapping Rodney back to reality. He leaned against the locker next to Rodney's. "What's up? You look like you've seen a ghost."

"Ally," Rodney stammered, his voice shaking. "She admitted she had feelings for me, but she's still choosing Matt."

"Whoa," Derek said, his eyebrows shooting up. "That's… wow, man, congrats on getting her to admit that!"

"Congrats?" Rodney's brow furrowed, frustration bubbling beneath the surface. "She just wants to be friends because she thinks I'm dating Erica, but we're just friends."

"Hey, don't worry about it," Derek reassured him, clapping a hand on his shoulder. "Now that we know Ally has feelings for you, we can definitely get you two together by the end of the year. Trust me, it's clear the two of you are meant to be."

Rodney nodded slowly, trying to make sense of everything that just happened. In his mind's eye, he tried to picture himself with Ally, sitting across from her at a dimly lit restaurant. Their hands reached out and intertwined, fingers laced together like a perfect puzzle piece. As they leaned in for a kiss, anticipation crackling between them like electricity, Rodney blinked –And suddenly, it was Parker staring back at him, not Ally. The shock sent a jolt through his entire body, was Ally really who he wanted to be with anymore?

"Uh, so what's the next step?" Rodney asked, his voice betraying a hint of uncertainty.

Derek grinned, wrapping his arm around Rodney as he finished zipping up his backpack. "First, we say you and Erica broke up and you are really heartbroken about it. Then, Ally comes and comforts you, and the next thing you know you are falling for each other. Trust me, man – we've got this."

As they walked away, Rodney couldn't help but feel a mixture of hope and unease. The thought of being with Ally filled him was a dream come true, but so did the thought of being with Parker. It was a puzzle he couldn't quite decipher, but for now, he had to focus on winning Ally's heart.

8

I

The school cafeteria buzzed with the usual chatter and laughter as Rodney dissected his turkey sandwich, his appetite lost in the sea of his anxious thoughts. Ally had been avoiding him ever since she confessed she had feelings for him at one point, and even after he faked the breakup with Erica, she never reached out.

"Rodney, man," Derek said, pulling him from his thoughts. "She's just figuring things out. Give it time. After the holidays, I bet everything will go back to normal."

"Easy for you to say," Rodney mumbled. He appreciated Derek's optimism, but right now, he needed a dose of reality more than anything. "What if she didn't mean all that stuff about staying friends? What if she was just trying to let me down gently?"

"Trust me," Derek said, stealing the turkey of Rodney's sandwich. "Best friends never really give up on each other. She'll come around."

"Thanks, Derek." Rodney offered a half-hearted smile before gathering his lunch tray and heading to class.

As Derek watched Rodney shuffle out of the cafeteria, he overheard Madison complaining animatedly to Chelsea. "Can you believe Ally's throwing an ugly holiday sweater party? I wanted to look cute for the party, not like a walking disaster!"

"Hey, it'll be fun! She has a 50-dollar gift card to Starbucks as a prize for the ugliest sweater" Chelsea replied, her excitement evident. "Besides, it's just one night."

Derek's eyes narrowed as realization struck – Rodney hadn't been invited. He knew something had to be done, and fast or Rodney would be heartbroken.

———-

After school, Derek caught up with Rodney. "Hey, could you help me pick out a Christmas gift at the bookstore for my mom?" he asked, feigning desperation.

"Sure." Rodney agreed, puzzled. "But I thought your mom hated reading?"

"Ah, well," Derek hesitated, rubbing the back of his neck. "She doesn't hate it, she just avoids it at all costs." Rodney laughed and the pair headed out.

They arrived at Readmore Second Hand Bookstore, and Rodney's confusion only deepened. But before he could question Derek's motives, he bumped into Ally's mom, Tara.

"Rodney! What a pleasure seeing you here, it feels like ages since you have been over," Tara greeted them warmly. "Isn't Strathroy a wonderful town? Full of history, perfect for my book."

"Uh, yeah," Rodney stumbled, his face flushing as he tried to mirror her enthusiasm. "It's definitely... interesting."

"Speaking of interesting," Derek interjected smoothly. "I'm Derek and I can't wait for Ally's ugly sweater party. Sounds like a blast!"

"Wait, there's a party?" Rodney asked, his eyes widening in surprise.

"You mean you haven't heard about the party?" Tara exclaimed, taken aback. "I thought Ally invited you. She must have been so busy planning it that she forgot. Here are the details." She scribbled down the details on a Post-it from her purse. "Sometimes I swear that girl would lose her head if it wasn't screwed on tight."

"Thanks, Mrs. Matthews." Rodney managed a smile as he tucked the note away.

"I can't believe Ally was throwing an ugly sweater party and didn't invite me, wait was this your plan all along?" Rodney huffed as he and Derek left the shop, Derek simply nodded. "How did you even know Ally's mom would be here?"

"Easy," Derek grinned, pulling out his phone. "I followed Tara on Instagram. That woman practically lives on it."

"Thanks, man," Rodney said sincerely. "This could be my chance to fix things with Ally." After a quick hug, the duo went their separate ways.

———-

Later that evening Rodney found Marcy studying at the Kitchen table. "Marcy, can you help me make an ugly sweater for Ally's party?" Rodney asked, holding up a plain green sweater he found buried deep in his closet.

"Sure thing," Marcy replied, her freckled face lighting up with excitement. "It beats doing math equations and I've got the perfect idea for a truly hideous sweater."

Together, they spent hours sewing plastic ornaments and tinsel onto the old green sweater until it looked like a horribly decorated Christmas tree. The once-plain fabric was now adorned with mismatched baubles, garish tinsel, and blinking fairy lights that Marcy had discovered at the bottom of their holiday decorations box.

"Wow, this is truly hideous," Rodney said, beaming with pride as he held up their creation. "Thanks for helping me, Marcy."

"Anytime," she replied, grinning widely. "If this isn't the ugliest sweater you've ever seen then I don't know what is," She returned to her textbook and Rodney raced the sweater to its new home at the front of his closet.

———-

The day of the party arrived, and Marcy dropped Rodney off at Ally's house. As he walked up to the front door, he could hear the lively conversations of guests inside. Taking a deep breath, he entered and immediately felt like he'd been transported to a winter wonderland.

The living room was decked out in twinkling lights, and there was a sugar cookie decorating contest happening in one corner, while a group of kids played pass-the-present in another. Winter-themed treats were laid out on tables, and a large inflatable Santa dominated the centre of the room.

Rodney barely had time to take it all in when a flash went off in his face. Blinking away the spots in his vision, he saw Madison grinning behind a Polaroid camera.

"Sorry, Rodney! I'm taking pictures for the vote on who has the ugliest sweater," she explained, snapping another photo as he squinted at her. She gave him a once-over, her eyes narrowing as she took in the abomination he wore. "You're definitely the front-runner right now."

"Uh, thanks?" Rodney said, unsure whether to feel flattered or insulted. "Do you know where Ally is?"

"Somewhere in the house," Madison shrugged, already losing interest as she spotted another guest with an impressively ugly sweater. "You'll find her eventually."

"Helpful," Rodney muttered under his breath, feeling a mix of anticipation and anxiety at seeing Ally again. As he ventured deeper into the party, he couldn't help but wonder how their encounter would unfold, and whether coming to this party was really a good idea.

As he rounded the stairs to the basement, Rodney felt a swell of pride as people complimented his sweater and took photos with him. The tinsel twinkled from the fairy lights, and the plastic ornaments jingled with every step he took. Amidst the laughter and conversations, he caught the sound of Ally's voice and followed it toward a cluster of party-goers sitting in a circle, playing truth or dare.

As soon as Ally spotted Rodney, she left Matt's side and strode over to him, her face a mix of surprise and concern. "Rodney, I didn't know you were coming," she said, glancing between him and the monstrosity he wore.

"Your mom invited me," he replied, trying to sound casual. "I thought maybe you just forgot with everything else going on."

Ally paused for a moment, biting her lip before nodding. "Yeah, I'm so sorry. I've been really busy planning this party and… I guess I just forgot." She gave him a weak smile, but the awkward silence that hung between them was quickly shattered when Jordan breezed into the room and threw an arm around Rodney's shoulders.

"Is this the legendary holiday disaster I've heard so much about?" they exclaimed, eyeing Rodney's sweater with delight. "Looks like what would happen if a drugged-up arsonist tried to decorate a tree. I am here for it!"

"Thanks, I think?" Rodney replied, unable to suppress a grin.

"Seriously, dude, that thing's epic!" Luke chimed in, joining the group. He clapped Rodney on the back, making the ornaments jingle even louder.

From the corner of his eye, Rodney noticed Matt watching them, his jaw clenched and eyebrows furrowed. Seeming unable to hold back any longer, Matt approached Rodney with a scowl. "I couldn't tell the difference between that sweater and what you normally wear," he sniped.

"Matt, that's uncalled for and a jerk move," Ally snapped, her eyes flashing with annoyance. She looked between Rodney and Matt, her chest heaving as if the air in the room had suddenly grown thin. Overwhelmed, she turned and fled up the stairs.

Rodney instinctively moved to follow her, but Luke grabbed his arm, shaking his head. "Let them sort it out, man. You don't want to get involved in their lovers' quarrel."

As Matt disappeared after Ally, Rodney couldn't help but worry about how he may have just ruined the party for Ally. He tried to focus on the fun around him, but his thoughts kept straying back to Ally, and the awkward distance between them that just seemed to get wider every day.

Rodney made his way to the bathroom, his head spinning with negative thoughts. He locked the door behind him and leaned against it, taking a deep breath as he tried to talk himself down, he could just go home and spare Ally any more trouble. As he reached for the door, his phone buzzed in his pocket.

"Ally?" he whispered, surprised to see her name flash across the screen. It was an incoming call. His finger hovered over the decline button, but then he hesitated. Maybe she was calling because she wanted to talk about everything that had happened or even better, because she had broken up with Matt. With a shaky hand, he swiped to accept the call and pressed the phone to his ear.

"Matt, you're smothering me!" Ally's voice rang out, clearly upset. Rodney realized at that moment it must have been a pocket dial, but he couldn't bring himself to hang up.

"Ally, I'm just trying to protect you," Matt's voice responded defensively.

"From who exactly? why don't you just say it!" Ally pushed.

"Rodney, you know he is after you right? He is always just trying to get with you" Matt said, and Rodney's heart dropped.

"Rodney is harmless, and I am allowed to be friends with whoever I want!" It was clear Ally was frustrated by Matt's accusations.

"I am just doing this because I love you," Matt countered.

"By hovering over me and trying to control my every move? That's not love, Matt. That's control."

Rodney listened intently, his stomach churning with anxiety as the argument unfolded. He knew he shouldn't have heard any of this, and guilt caused him to hang up.

"Deep breaths," Rodney muttered to himself, trying to regain his composure. He unlocked the door and stepped back into the party, deciding it was better for him to just go home. As he headed to the front door someone bumped into him from behind.

"Hey, Rodney! We have to stop meeting like this," Parker's voice greeted him, as he held Rodney steady. Parker was wearing a sweater featuring a purple alien cat playing an electric guitar, which just seemed to make the gold flecks in his eyes shimmer.

"Wow, that sweater of yours is… unique," Rodney stammered, wondering why Parker seemed so cool with him after their falling out a few weeks ago.

"Thanks! Your sweater is pretty epic too," Parker replied with a grin, and for the first time since that night began, Rodney felt a flicker of genuine happiness. They exchanged awkward glances, unsure of what to say next.

"Is it just me or is this living room feeling a bit cramped with all these people in it, do you want to go get some air with me?" Parker finally suggested, motioning toward the door.

'That would be amazing," Rodney agreed, grateful for the escape, and they stepped outside into the gently falling snow.

As they walked side by side, Parker asked "I have been meaning to ask you something for a while now, you lied that time you told me you didn't love Ally, right? I was just wondering because the two of you act so differently around each other. Like it couldn't be anything else, I was just wondering when this whole thing started?" Rodney wasn't sure if it was the cold or not but Parker almost seemed sad asking the question.

Rodney hesitated "Last year I lost my dad, in a car accident on his way home from work. I went to a really dark place, but Ally never left me, even when most of my other friends stopped coming around or asking to hang out. I know I wasn't that fun to be around but she helped a lot, dragging me to places and trying to make me smile. I knew then I loved her, I just wasn't ready to tell her yet."

"Oh wow, I am sorry. I know losing someone is never easy, my brother was born with a heart defect, and I only knew him for two weeks. I still think about him a lot though, mom still hangs a stocking for him at Christmas." Parker stopped and looked up at the sky. "All I can say is it gets easier in time, more good than bad days"

Rodney pulled Parker into a hug, an automatic response to his story and feeling like someone finally got him "I had no idea, I am so sorry for your loss."

"Isn't it funny how we can share these things with each other?" Parker mused, smiling softly at Rodney. "I guess those with shared trauma just get each other," he said half-jokingly, in an attempt to lighten the mood.

Rodney laughed, nodding in agreement "It's getting pretty cold out, do you want to go get a hot chocolate with me?" Rodney asked, still feeling the warmth from their hug.

"Good idea, if I get any colder I might end up losing a toe," Parker joked. As they walked through the snow, silent but content, Rodney couldn't help but imagine kissing Parker again under the mistletoe. The thought made him feel as warm as their hug did, and he wondered how he could feel the same way about Parker that he did about Ally.

9

Don't

Ally stood in her living room, hands on her hips, surveying the hulking Pac-Man machine like a general regarding her troops. She had enlisted the help of Matt's closest friends - Parker, Steven, and Luke - to pull off the birthday surprise she was certain would prove once and for all just how well she knew her boyfriend, and make up for their fight at her party.

"Did Matt even ask for this?" Parker questioned, skeptically pushing up his glasses as he eyed the dusty arcade game.

"No," Ally admitted, brushing a strand of her long blonde hair behind her ear. "But as his girlfriend, I have to show how well I know him with a unique and personal gift." The boys exchanged glances before Steven spoke up.

"Getting this thing working again will be a lot of work, Ally. And there are so many things Matt asked for…maybe we should just stick to the list?"

"Matt loves video games and these old arcade machines," Ally insisted, patting the machine and causing a dust cloud to emerge from it. "Besides, he told me once that his favourite childhood memory was playing this game with his mom in the arcade in Niagara Falls."

Luke sighed, clearly touched by the sentiment. "That's the sweetest thing I've ever heard. Alright, I'm in." Steven nodded agreement, and after a moment's hesitation, Parker joined in as well, not wanting to be the odd one out.

———-

The next day at school, Rodney sat slumped over the cafeteria table, staring at the red 68 scrawled on his latest English essay. He'd never scored so low on anything in his life, and panic gnawed at his insides like a rabid squirrel.

"Rodney, it's just an essay," Derek said, reading over his shoulder. "Madison and I have done way worse."

"Exactly," Madison chimed in, flipping her brown hair over her shoulder. "You'll bounce back."

"Guys, I've never gotten lower than an 85 on anything," Rodney confessed, unable to look at them. Their expressions of shock mirrored his own disbelief. "I spent hours researching this, I thought it was perfect."

"Alright," Derek said, cracking his knuckles. "Let's find out what happened."

As the trio decided to pay Rodney's teacher a visit, Ally and her team of fixer-uppers laboured over the Pac-Man machine after school, determined to bring it back to life in time for Matt's birthday.

Ally's hands were a blur of nimble fingers as she worked to snap some of the missing buttons into place, her determination fueled by the thought of their fight. Luke, Steven, and Parker hunched over the project with her, trying to concentrate on the tutorial video they had found online.

"Okay," Ally said, wiping her brow with the back of her hand. "Let's take a break for a minute." She glanced around at their tired faces and decided to try taking their minds off the work. "So, I was wondering… What's the nicest thing you guys have ever done for a past girlfriend?"

Steven chuckled. "In grade eight, I volunteered to be Missy Dawson's model for an art class. Didn't realize I'd be modelling a dress she made, though." He grinned sheepishly. "But hey, I wore the crap out of it."

Laughter bubbled up from the group, as Parker and Luke remembered the moment. It was Parker's turn next. "Well, I've never actually dated anyone," he admitted, his voice tinged with embarrassment. "But the nicest thing I've ever done for someone I liked was stepping aside so they could be with the person they really wanted."

Luke snorted. "That's lame. How do you even know they wouldn't be happy with you?"

Parker's face flushed crimson. "I just… know," he mumbled, his gaze fixed on the floor.

"Alright, Luke, what about you?" Ally asked, trying to steer the conversation away from Parker's discomfort.

"Uh, let's see…" Luke scratched his head, deep in thought. "I guess the nicest thing I've ever done for a girl, was buy her a lemonade."

Parker rolled his eyes. "This is why you're single, man."

"Hey, it was an expensive lemonade! It had real strawberries and everything!" Luke protested, crossing his arms defensively.

As the banter continued, they all returned to the Pac-Man machine. After a few more minutes of tinkering, they stood back and prepared to plug the machine in. To their surprise, the machine hummed to life, its familiar jingle resounding triumphantly through the garage.

——-

The next morning, Rodney squared his shoulders as he entered Mr. Greenburg's classroom after school, Derek's pep talk still echoing in his ears. "Mr. Greenburg, can we talk about my grade on the essay?"

His teacher peered at him over his glasses. "Ah, yes. I remember your paper. It wasn't your best work, Rodney."

Rodney swallowed hard. "I know, sir, but a 68? I know it wasn't that bad. Is there any way I could get another chance?"

Mr. Greenburg shook his head, his expression unyielding. "I expected more from you, so I marked you more harshly. Learn from it and move on." He pointed Rodney toward the door.

With that dismissal, Rodney left the classroom, he would never fight what a teacher told him. He relayed the conversation to Derek and Madison, who were outraged. They exchanged knowing glances, silently agreeing that Mr. Greenburg had crossed a line – and it was time to seek their revenge.

——-

The evening sun dipped below the horizon, Ally paced excitedly in Matt's living room. Matt's birthday party was about to begin, and all his friends had already gathered at his house, waiting to surprise him. She could feel her heart racing with anticipation, certain that he would love the gift she'd spent days working on.

"Okay, everyone! He's almost here!" Ally whispered, after reading a text from Matt's mom. The room fell silent as they all hid behind furniture and held their breaths.

The front door creaked open, and Matt stepped inside, completely unaware of the surprise waiting for him. In unison, the group leaped out from their hiding spots, shouting, "Surprise!"

Matt's eyes widened in shock, and then a grin spread across his face. He rushed over to Ally, pulling her into a passionate kiss. "Thank you Ally Cat, this party looks amazing," he laughed, looking around at his friends.

"Wait, there's more," Ally said, taking his hand. She led Matt to the garage, where the freshly restored Pac-Man machine stood proudly against the wall. The moment felt perfect – until she saw Matt's face.

"Wow, Ally, this must have cost a fortune. I can't accept this," he said, running a hand through his hair, his smile faltering.

"It wasn't too bad," she reassured him, trying to gauge his thoughts. "Don't worry about the cost."

"But I don't really have a place for it," Matt mumbled, glancing around the garage.

"Your dad said you can keep it out here," Ally replied, forcing a smile. But deep down, she couldn't shake the feeling that she had messed up. Matt's smile seemed forced, and she began to think maybe she didn't know him as well as she thought she did.

"Thanks, Ally. It's… thoughtful." His words hung in the air, and Ally's heart sank a little.

———-

Meanwhile, under the cloak of darkness, Rodney and Madison stood outside an old home, shivering slightly in the night air. Rodney's brow furrowed in confusion. "Why are we here, Madison?"

"Revenge," she whispered, revealing a carton of eggs and a roll of toilet paper. "This is Mr. Greenburg's house."

Rodney hesitated for a moment, weighing the consequences. But as he remembered the sting of his undeserved grade and reached for the carton. Together, they began their assault on the teacher's home, pelting it with eggs and draping toilet paper over every possible surface.

The thrill of retribution coursed through Rodney's veins – that is until the piercing sound of police sirens shattered the night. Panic took hold as Madison sprinted away, leaving Rodney to stumble over a bush in his haste to escape. The world seemed to slow down as he tumbled to the ground, knowing he'd been caught.

"Son, you're coming with us," said the stern-faced officer as he escorted Rodney back to his house. His mother was waiting for him, disappointment etched into her features. She didn't say a word, simply gesturing for him to go to bed.

———-

"Seriously? Rodney did that?" Ally asked, barely able to conceal her shock and curiosity as Parker recounted the events on Monday.

"Yep. Egged Mr. Greenburg's house because of a bad grade," Parker confirmed with a smile, pushing his glasses up the bridge of his nose.

Ally shook her head, strands of her long blonde hair dancing around her face. "Wow. I never would have expected that from him." A glimmer of admiration flickered in her eyes before she hastily added, "Not that I condone it or anything."

"Of course not," Parker agreed, shaking his head but his smile remained plastered onto his face. "I should get going, but I just thought you'd want to know."

"Thanks, Parker," Ally said, watching him walk away. She felt an uncharacteristic urge to share the news with Matt even though he wasn't Rodney's biggest fan; perhaps it was the novelty of Rodney's rebellious act or maybe since she felt she couldn't talk to Rodney about it, Matt was the safer option.

Ally made her way to the gym and spotted Matt on the court, talking animatedly to Jordan. As she neared, Ally's steps slowed, her ears catching snippets of their conversation.

"…sold the Pac-man machine – got enough cash to buy everything else on my birthday list," Matt boasted, as he went in for a layup.

"Man, what's Ally gonna say when she finds out?" Jordan asked, concern etched on their face.

"Relax," Matt shrugged, a smug grin spreading across his features. "Ally won't find out. We never hang out in my garage."

Ally's heart shattered, her earlier joy obliterated by an overwhelming tsunami of sorrow. She fought back tears, silently retreating before they could spot her eavesdropping.

———-

Rodney fidgeted nervously in the school psychologist's office, unsure of what to expect. The door swung open and Mr. Rogo entered, a kind smile on his face.

"Hello, Rodney," he greeted warmly. "I understand you've been having some difficulties adjusting to your new school environment. I'm here to help, tell me what's going on, I am sure we can find a solution."

"How do you plan on doing that?" Rodney asked skeptically, his fingers tapping a restless rhythm on the armrests of his chair.

"By listening," Mr. Rogo replied gently, taking a seat opposite Rodney. "You can start anything you want – just tell me what's on your mind."

Rodney hesitated for a moment before launching into the story of his move to Strathroy, his voice growing more confident as he recounted his feelings about everything that had happened. But when he was about to discuss the mix of emotions he had been feeling about Parker, he faltered, pausing just long enough to catch himself.

"...Ally and Madison," he added hastily, avoiding Mr. Rogo's perceptive gaze. "Is it possible to have romantic feelings for more than one person?"

Mr. Rogo leaned back in his chair, nodding thoughtfully. "It's not uncommon, especially at your age. Emotions can be complex and confusing, but they're also an important part of who we are. Why don't we continue this discussion tomorrow."

10

Know

The following day, after school, Rodney spotted Derek leaning against the red brick wall, chatting with a group of his other friends. He hoped to tell Derek about his mom's video game ban for the month, but as he began walking towards him, his mother's firm hand on his shoulder stopped him.

"Rodney, we're going home right now," Sasha said sternly, her eyes scanning over the scene like a hawk. "I can't trust you to use your free time wisely."

"Mom…" Rodney's voice trailed off when she shot him a look, annoyance and frustration simmering beneath the surface. He swallowed the words he wanted to say, knowing that it would only make things worse to fight her on this. Instead, he gave a resigned nod and followed her to the car.

As they sat side by side in silence, Rodney wished his dad was still there to crack a terrible joke and give him a warning like he used to. But he was gone, and Rodney felt like he lost the one person who really understood him.

When they got home, the kitchen was a battleground, the air thick with tension as Sasha stood before her son, arms folded tightly across her chest. Her eyes narrowed dangerously, and she gritted her teeth as she spoke. "So, I have been giving what you did a lot of thought," her disappointment clear.

Rodney shifted his weight from one foot to another, his gaze darting around the room as he waited for the new punishment. He sighed, finally meeting his mother's stare. "I said I was sorry" he explained reluctantly. "But, Mom, he wouldn't even give me another chance and I didn't deserve that grade."

His voice cracked with frustration and pleaded for understanding.

He didn't mention that he felt like Ally had abandoned him. He also kept quiet about the confusing feelings he'd been having towards Parker lately. His mother already had enough ammunition against him; there was no need to provide more.

"Whether the grade was fair or not, I expect more from you, Rodney." Sasha's voice grew cold, her disappointment clear. "This is unacceptable behaviour."

"Fine, I won't stand up for myself next time," he muttered, averting his eyes again. He knew better than to argue when his mother had that particular edge to her tone.

Sasha crossed her arms, not impressed with Rodney's sarcastic response. "You're grounded until the end of the semester," she declared, her voice as unwavering as her decision.

"Grounded?" Rodney's eyebrows shot up in disbelief. "But I said I wouldn't do it again!"

"And I believe you as much as any mother can believe a teenage boy," Sasha retorted sharply, her eyes narrowing. "You can use this time to focus on your school work. Eighties aren't hundreds."

Rodney clenched his jaw, his frustration mounting. He wanted to argue further, but he knew it would be futile. Instead, he nodded curtly and retreated to his room, slamming the door behind him. As he sat down at his desk and pulled out his textbooks, his mind raced with thoughts of unfairness and injustice and how if his dad had been here none of this would have been happening.

Later that night, Sasha left the house to pick up a few things, her heels clicking briskly on the pavement. As she pushed her cart through the grocery store aisles, she rounded a corner and nearly collided with Tara. Her heart sank, a mixture of surprise and dread settling in her stomach.

"Hello, Sasha!" Tara greeted her warmly, with open arms. "Fancy running into you here!"

"Hi, Tara." Sasha forced a smile and leaned in for the awkward hug. She hadn't known that Ally's family had also moved to Strathroy. "What brings you to town?"

"Didn't Rodney tell you?" Tara asked, her blue eyes sparkling. "We moved here because I'm writing a book, and I needed to research some local history for the mystery plot. Plus, we thought it'd be great for Rodney and Ally to be in high school together since they were practically raised together."

"Ah, yes, it would have been a shame if they were apart," Sasha murmured, feigning agreement. Internally, she bristled at the thought of Rodney being weighed down by Ally, who she saw as a hindrance to his academic potential. "That's… wonderful."

"Isn't it?" Tara beamed, utterly oblivious to Sasha's true feelings. "Well, I'd better get going, dinner isn't going to cook itself. See you around!"

"Bye, Tara," Sasha said tightly, watching her walk away before resuming her shopping.

As she filled her cart with groceries, Sasha couldn't shake the nagging worry that Ally was the reason Rodney had been acting out, egging a house would be one of her schemes. She resolved to keep a closer eye on Rodney, determined to protect her son from anything – or anyone – that might hold him back.

———

The warm aroma of roasted meat filled the air as Sasha entered the house, her arms laden with grocery bags. Rodney glanced up from his homework, watching as she set about setting the table and putting the groceries away.

"Guess who I ran into at the store?" Sasha asked nonchalantly as she placed glasses at each place setting.

"Who?" Rodney replied, his pencil tapping nervously against the table.

"Ally's mother, Tara," she said, her tone tinged with disapproval. "She mentioned that Ally is in some of your classes. Why didn't you tell me?"

Rodney shifted uneasily in his seat. "I didn't think it was important."

Marcy, who had been watching the roast, knew what was about to happen and tried to intervene. "Hey, let's just enjoy dinner, okay? We can talk about this later." But her words did little to calm the storm that was brewing.

"Rodney," Sasha said, setting down the plated roast, "It was Ally who convinced you to egg that teacher's house wasn't it."

For a moment, the dining room seemed to transform into a courtroom,

Sasha questioning Rodney at the stand, trying to get the evidence she wanted. He rolled his eyes at the accusation, hands gripping the edge of the table tightly.

"Ally had nothing to do with it," he insisted, his voice firm. "I made my own choice."

"Really?" Sasha countered, raising an eyebrow. "Was she not the one who convinced you to use the old rope swing by the lake? You ended up with your arm broken in two places."

"Mom, that was an accident and we were nine," Rodney retorted, closing his book.

"Maybe so, but your grades suffered because of that incident," Sasha continued, her voice cold and accusatory. "Her childish schemes always come back to bite you, not her."

"It was because I couldn't write with a cast and our teacher was too busy dealing with the kid throwing desks to help me," Rodney exclaimed, his cheeks flushing with anger. "You have always just hated Ally because you don't think she is as smart as me."

"Rodney–" Marcy tried to interject, but he cut her off.

"Mom, you don't really care about me," Rodney said, struggling to keep his voice from trembling. "All you care about is our family's image. Well, guess what our family is broken, Dad is gone and we never seem to talk about that. Like if we just ignore it, it didn't happen."

The words hung heavy in the air, a painful truth that couldn't be unsaid. The once-inviting aroma of the roast now seemed suffocating, filling the room with oppressive heat. And for a moment, everything stood still.

Rodney looked around at his family, their faces a mixture of shock and sadness. Marcy reached out a hand as if to comfort him, but he pulled away.

"Mom, you only ever seemed to listen to Dad," he continued, tears streaming down his face. "We're all hurting, but it feels like you don't want to hear it."

With that, Rodney stormed from the table, the clatter of his chair hitting the floor echoing through the suddenly quiet room.

Rodney slammed his bedroom door shut behind him, the harsh sound reverberating off the walls like a physical weight. Leaning against the door, he let out a ragged breath and wiped angrily at his tear-streaked cheeks.

He needed a distraction – anything to take his mind off the painful confrontation he'd just left. Pulling his phone from his pocket, Rodney began scrolling through stories, desperate for something to ease the raw ache in his chest.

Then, he saw it: Parker's newest update. A photo of Parker and Madison together, standing in front of a massive Christmas tree. The caption beneath it read, "The best gift is a new relationship." His heart clenched painfully, and a wave of sadness washed over him. Seeing Parker with Madison hurt him the same way seeing Ally with Matt did, even if he didn't quite know why.

"Damn it," he muttered, switching off his phone and tossing it into his laundry basket with more force than necessary.

Outside his bedroom door, Sasha stood hesitating, her hand raised as if to knock. She wanted to say something – anything – to address the painful words her son had spoken at dinner. But she didn't know how to apologize, or even where to begin.

She lingered there, her heart aching with the knowledge that she had failed her son in so many ways.

"Rodney," she whispered, her voice barely audible even to herself, "I'm so sorry."

But the door remained closed, and the distance between them only seemed to grow.

11

What

The heavy silence in the cafeteria was finally broken by a collective exhale as the first semester finals drew to a close. Rodney sat alone at a table, tapping an idle rhythm on the cold plastic surface while he waited for Derek to finish emptying his locker. He had been grounded for what felt like an eternity, and now that he was free at last and eager to make up for lost time.

"Come on Derek, hurry up," Rodney whispered to himself, trying to ignore the laughter coming from a nearby table. His gaze flickered over to the source of the sound, finding Ally, Matt, Luke, Steven, and Parker all sitting together in a tight circle, their faces glowing with relief and excitement. Since being grounded, he hadn't really talked to any of them for weeks. He didn't exactly feel bad about it, since Parker and Ally were both busy with their significant others anyway.

Then, in the midst of their animated conversation, Matt's eyes locked onto Rodney's. Caught staring, Rodney quickly averted his gaze, focusing intently on the patterned linoleum floor beneath his feet. A bead of sweat trickled down the back of his neck, and he prayed that Matt wouldn't make a big deal about it.

"Hey guys!" Ally exclaimed, her voice ringing in the nearly empty cafeteria. "We should have a movie night to celebrate the end of exams! My place, tonight?"

"Sounds great," Steven agreed, adjusting his hoodie strings with a smile.

"Can I bring Madison?" Parker asked hesitantly.

"Sorry, Parker," Ally replied, biting her lip. "My parents are in Toronto, and they told me I can only have four friends over."

Rodney continued to stare at the ground, but he was very aware of the conversation happening next to him, he wished he could make himself invisible. He could still feel Matt's gaze on him, making his skin crawl. He knew Matt didn't like him, and he knew the gears were turning in Matt's head to make Ally feel the same way and ensure there really was nothing between them.

"Hey," Matt said suddenly, standing up at his table. "Why don't we invite Rodney? I mean didn't you say earlier, Ally, that he had been grounded until the end of the semester, well the semester's over right?"

"Really?" Ally asked, looking at Matt with surprise. Inviting Rodney was the last thing she had expected from her boyfriend. "You would be ok with that?"

"Sure," Matt made his way over to Rodney's table, his eyes never leaving him. "I think he deserves to have some fun more than anyone. After all, egging Mr. Greenburg was epic."

"Alright," Ally agreed, nodding. She turned to face Rodney, who was instinctively leaning away from Matt. "Rodney, would you like to join us for a movie night at my place tonight?"

"Uh, yeah!" Rodney stammered, not sure what was really happening. "Oh but didn't you say you could only have four friends over."

"Don't be silly," Ally beamed, genuinely happy to see Matt trying to include Rodney in their plans. "You know my parents would make an exception for you."

"Thanks, Ally," Rodney replied, trying to keep his voice steady. A chance to talk to Ally and hang out again was more than Rodney could've hoped for. It was a chance to catch up on all the things he missed while grounded, but he still didn't know why Matt invited him.

———–

"Can you believe it?" Rodney exclaimed as he walked alongside Derek, their shadows stretched out over the cracked sidewalk. "I was invited to Ally's movie night!"

"Really?" Derek raised an eyebrow, a hint of suspicion in his voice. "But didn't you say it was Matt's idea?"

"Yup," Rodney replied, kicking an ice chunk off the sidewalk with the toe of his boot. "Maybe since I haven't been hanging around so much he isn't worried about Ally and I being together."

"Or maybe there's something else going on," Derek countered. "That's not how Matt works. Trust me."

"Have you ever told me why you don't like him?" Rodney asked, genuinely curious.

"Actually, I—" Derek began but was interrupted when Jordan appeared from around the corner, their short, dyed hair looking even bluer in the sunlight.

"Hey, guys!" Jordan called out, catching up to them. "Rumour has it there's a movie night at Ally's?"

"Uh, yeah," Rodney replied, scratching the back of his neck. "Were you invited?"

"Not officially, I overheard Steven talking about it," Jordan sighed, disappointment flickering across their face. "But I am having a little movie night of my own. If you two want to come — I make perfect nachos."

"Oh, sorry Jordan but I already told Ally I would go to hers," Rodney said, trying to let them down easily.

"No, it's cool," Jordan said, feigning nonchalance as they turned away. "Catch you guys later."

As Jordan disappeared around the next corner, Derek picked up where he left off. "So, Matt? Yeah, we have a history, our moms are like best friends. Anyway, when he was in second grade he killed my fish. Took them right out of the aquarium to quote-on-quote play with them. And it got worse last year I was up for captain on our hockey team, and he told the coach I broke his stick on purpose and was taking things from their bags. Coach believed him and kicked me from the team…"

"Wow," Rodney murmured, his eyes widening in surprise. "That is actually a crazy thing to do."

"Right, he put the stuff in my bag," Derek said, "So be careful tonight, ok? Matt doesn't stop until he gets what he wants," he gave Rodney a reassuring pat on the shoulder as they continued their walk.

—-

"Hey, Ally!" Parker called out as he and Steven walked into her living room. "Luke can't make it. He didn't clean his room like his mom asked."

"Alright," Ally said, visibly disappointed. "Well, we're watching a Fast and Furious marathon. So I hope you're ready for an all-nighter."

"Ah, of course," Steven chuckled, rolling his eyes as Parker smirked. "I take it Matt chose the entertainment this evening,"

"Who else? Oh, I brought some Mountain Dew Red for everyone," Parker announced, revealing the rare, discontinued soda with pride.

"Really?" Ally wrinkled her nose and winced at the drink. "Do you know the amount of sugar in that, Parker?"

"Hey, let's order pizza!" Steven interjected, watching Parker about to argue. "Everyone loves pizza, right?"

"Great idea," Ally agreed, her smile returning. "There is this place that does cauliflower crust nearby and Matt should be here any minute."

"Speak of the devil," Parker muttered under his breath as Matt swaggered into Ally's living room, fashionably late. "Traffic was a nightmare," he claimed with a dramatic sigh.

"Perfect timing," Steven said, eyeing Matt skeptically. "We were just about to order pizza."

"Fantastic," Matt replied, his eyes lighting up. He snatched the phone from Steven and immediately dialled his favourite place, acting as if he knew everyone's favourite pizzas by heart. "One pepperoni, one veggie, and one supreme —" he paused, smirking to himself, "—with extra cheese." He hung up before anyone got a word in.

As Matt placed the phone down, he casually removed his jacket, revealing that he wasn't wearing a shirt underneath. "Sweat through it at the gym," he explained nonchalantly, but Parker could tell he was just insecure about Rodney coming and trying to make a statement in the only way he seemed to know how.

"Hey, where's Rodney?" Matt inquired, feigning concern. "Thought he was joining us tonight?"

Ally frowned, slightly worried. "I don't know. He didn't really respond to my text."

Matt's lips curved into a satisfied smile at the thought of Rodney's absence. He pulled back on his jacket, faking a shiver.

The doorbell rang, and there stood Rodney, arms laden with grocery bags overflowing with every chip flavour imaginable. "Didn't know what everyone liked," he gasped, struggling to maintain his grip on the precarious load. "So I bought them all."

"Total power move, dude!" Steven grinned, rushing to help Rodney with the bags. Matt scowled, clearly irked by how easy it was for Rodney to make a good impression.

As they settled down in the living room and started the first movie, Rodney glanced around curiously. "The Fast and The Furious? I mean, it's fine, but —"

"Matt's favourite," Parker interrupted, looking over at Rodney.

"Ah," Rodney nodded, understanding. He noticed Parker sneaking a text to someone as the movie began, it must be Madison he thought. He kind of wished Parker was texting him through the slog of a film.

The doorbell rang, shattering the momentary calm that had settled over the room as the movie reached its second act. Parker leaped to his feet, pocketing his phone. "That must be the pizza," he announced, making a beeline for the door.

"Finally," Matt muttered, shifting restlessly on the white sofa. Rodney glanced at him warily, remembering Derek's warning about Matt always getting what he wanted.

Parker returned moments later, balancing a stack of pizza boxes and… Madison? Rodney blinked in surprise as Madison slipped past Parker with a sheepish smile, her presence an unexpected twist in the evening's events.

"Uh, what are you doing here?" Ally asked, her voice equal parts confusion and irritation.

"Hey, Ally! Parker invited me," Madison replied, casting him a sideways glance. "Since Luke couldn't make it, he said I could take his spot."

"Really, Parker?" Ally frowned, crossing her arms. "You could've at least given me a heads-up."

"Come on, Ally," Parker protested. "She is taking Luke's spot. No house rules broken, right?"

"Guys, enough!" Matt interjected, his face growing redder by the second. "You're making me miss the movie. Everyone's here, let's just enjoy it."

"Fine," Ally huffed, taking the pizza boxes and placing them on the glass coffee table. Madison took a seat beside Parker, who handed her a can of Mountain Dew Code Red with a grin. As the movie continued, Rodney could hear Parker's low grumbling as he complained to Madison about Ally's behaviour. "Every time she's around Matt, she turns into a control freak," Madison murmured soothing words, her hand rubbing Parker's arm.

The doorbell chimed once more, startling everyone in the room. Steven stood, shaking his head. "I'll get it this time."

He returned moments later, trailed by a casually dressed Jordan. "Hey, guys," Jordan greeted nonchalantly. "I was just in the neighbourhood and thought I'd pop by to see how Ally's doing."

"Nice cover story," Rodney thought, casting a knowing glance in Jordan's direction. He had to give Jordan points for getting into the movie night on their own.

"Sure, the more the merrier," Ally said with a forced smile, though her eyes betrayed her lingering irritation.

"Thanks!" Jordan beamed, taking a seat next to Steven. The two friends began whispering animatedly about workout routines, Jordan's eyes widening as Steven shared his recent progress with a flex. Rodney could hear traces of admiration in Jordan's voice as they marvelled at Steven's transformation.

Rodney leaned back, the scent of pizza wafting through the air as he tried to focus on the movie. But even amidst the high-speed chases and witty banter, he couldn't help but feel alone.

Looking around the room, Rodney couldn't help but notice how Madison and Parker were lost in their own world of whispered conversations and sipping Code Red, while Jordan and Steven engaged in an animated discussion about the merits of different workout routines. And, of course, there were Matt and Ally, sitting close together, his arm draped around her shoulders, but Rodney had no one.

At that moment, Rodney felt out of place and needed an escape. He retreated into a daydream where he was the center of attention, surrounded by adoring friends who celebrated him with a musical number. In this fantasy, Jordan, Madison, and Steven danced as energetic backup singers, while Parker, Matt, and Ally harmonized in a chorus, praising his virtues and singing of his undeniable charm. Each of them was genuinely happy to be around him.

"Rodney! Hey, Rodney!"

The sound of his name jolted Rodney back to reality, and he blinked, refocusing on the present. He found himself staring at Parker and Ally, who were arguing once again, their voices raised in frustration. Madison looked over at Rodney, her eyebrows furrowed in concern. "You should do something," she urged, gesturing toward the two friends at each other's throats.

"Why me?" Rodney asked.

"Because it's about you," Madison informed him.

Before Rodney could utter a word, Ally snapped, "Rodney was my friend first, you know. We used to do everything together and now you come along and he spends all his time with you."

Parker scoffed, rolling his eyes. "Ally, you did that to yourself by ignoring him." Rodney stood there, feeling exposed and bewildered as to how this argument had become about him.

"Enough!" Matt shouted suddenly, silencing both Ally and Parker. All eyes turned to him as he continued, "You two were great friends, and now all you do is fight. And it's always about one thing... Rodney," His accusing gaze settled on Rodney, who suddenly noticed all eyes were on him. "Obviously, he's the problem."

A sinking feeling twisted in Rodney's gut as he realized that Matt was using Ally and Parker against him – Rodney didn't know what to do or say to get out of this. The room went quiet as they all stared at him, waiting for a response.

"Uh hey, I don't want to see friends fighting. My dad and I used to play music together, after every time we had a fight or an argument. It really helped ease the tension," Rodney grabbed Mark's guitar off the wall and began strumming the chords to *'Lips of an Angel.'* He poured his heart into the performance, his voice soaring as he sang the poignant lyrics, hoping to distract from the argument.

When he finished, there was a moment of silence as the group was bewildered by what had just occurred before Matt sneered, "Trying to seduce my girlfriend now, are you?"

"Of course not! No, I was just trying to…" Rodney protested, but it was too late. Matt stormed out of the room, followed by Steven and Jordan, who tried to calm him down. Parker left with Madison in tow, muttering about needing space from Ally.

Feeling like he'd only made things worse, Rodney slumped back onto the couch, ready to pack up and leave. But then Ally placed her hand on his shoulder, her touch gentle and comforting. "I remember when your dad taught you that song so you could play it with him," she said softly. "You've always had a way with music, Rodney."

She sat down beside him, her blue eyes radiating warmth. "I miss him too," she admitted. "But I also miss the times we shared, like when he took us to Toronto Island, and we ate so much ice cream that I got sick on the ferry ride back." A faint smile crossed her lips at the memory. "You don't have to feel alone, Rodney. You'll always have me." Then she stood up and headed to talk to Matt.

As her words washed over him, Rodney knew she was the one. She knew exactly what to say and exactly how he was feeling when nobody else could. It had never been more clear to him that he loved her.

—-

As Derek's car pulled up in front of Ally's house, Rodney stepped out onto the sidewalk, feeling the cool night air brush against his face like an old friend. Before he could even close the door, Derek rolled down the window and leaned over the console.

"Hey man, how'd it go?" Derek asked, his voice tinged with curiosity and concern.

Rodney hesitated for a moment, the weight of the evening still heavy on his shoulders. He glanced back at the house, the flickering glow of the television visible through the living room window. "It was… interesting," he finally said, sliding into the passenger seat and shutting the door behind him.

"Interesting?" Derek raised an eyebrow as he pulled away from the curb. "That's one word for it. Care to elaborate?"

As they drove through the quiet streets, Rodney recounted the events of the movie night – from Matt's manipulations to the impromptu performance that had made everything worse. Derek listened intently, his grip on the steering wheel tightening as Rodney told him about Matt's reaction.

"Man, I wish I could have been there to witness it all," Derek muttered, shaking his head in disbelief. "You sure you're okay?"

Rodney nodded, staring out at the passing houses. "I'm fine, just… surprised, I guess. But there's something else, too." He hesitated, then continued, "When Ally and I talked after everyone left, she knew exactly what I needed to hear. And I think… I know now more than ever she is the one for me."

"Really?" Derek shot him a sidelong glance, a mischievous grin spreading across his face. "Well, it does say a lot that she checked in on you first."

"Does it?" Rodney asked, skepticism lacing his voice. "I mean, with everything that's happened, is it really the right time to be feeling this way, I mean it's not like she broke up with him,"

"Hey," Derek said, his tone growing serious. "There's never a 'right' time for feelings – they happen when they happen. And if you ask me, it sounds like Ally may still have some of those feelings for you too."

Rodney mulled over Derek's words, was it possible they both still had feelings for each other? "You really think there could still be something between us."

"Of course, man." Derek flashed him a reassuring smile. "Now, let's focus on getting you and Ally back on track, okay? If I recall correctly the original plan was you two lovebirds would be together by the end of the year."

"That's only five months away, is that enough time?" Rodney worried, thinking about just how optimistic his original timeline was.

"More than enough time buddy, we got this," Derek's certainty gave Rodney hope that he wouldn't feel so alone by the end of June.

12

To

The winter carnival at SDCI was in full swing, and the air buzzed with excitement and laughter. Snowflakes gently fell from the cloud-filled sky, softly kissing the noses of students as they darted between booths. Rodney stood beside Derek, his breath visible in the cold air. He'd never imagined he'd be looking forward to a school event, but the anticipation of spending the day with Derek and participating in the festivities had him practically bouncing on the balls of his feet.

"Man, this is going to be great!" Derek said as they walked through the carnival together. "Have you ever done a snow race before?"

"Can't say that I have," Rodney admitted, watching other teens stumble over themselves as they raced. Thoughts of bumping into Ally lingered in his mind, but today, he was determined to just have fun. "But there's a first time for everything, right?"

"Exactly!" Derek grinned. Together, they found their way to the snow race starting line, joining a small group of eager participants. The race was simple enough: run from one end of the designated area to the other, all while avoiding obstacles made of snow and ice. Rodney could feel his heart pounding in his chest as he crouched down, ready to sprint.

"Ready?" the volunteer shouted, and everyone nodded. "Set... Go!" In an instant, Rodney was off, adrenaline surging through his veins. His feet slipped and slid in the snow, but somehow, he managed to keep his balance. Laughter bubbled up inside him as he watched Derek stumble and fall over a snowman, only to pick himself up and continue racing, a look of pure determination on his face.

In the end, neither Rodney nor Derek won the race, but it hardly mattered. They were both grinning from ear to ear, their breaths coming in short, frosty puffs. "That was harder than expected," Rodney declared, high-fiving Derek.

"Hey, you did it, buddy," Derek said, grinning broadly. "Now I don't know about you, but I need to refuel, food?"

"Food." Rodney agreed.

As they wandered through the carnival, in search of the food stands, Rodney couldn't help but feel a little lighter. For once, he wasn't overthinking everything, and it felt like a weight had been lifted.

————-

As Rodney and Derek passed the Beaver Tail booth, they noticed Jordan and Steven were hard at work—or at least, that's what they wanted people to think. In reality, they were engaged in a full-on food fight, lobbing bits of dough and toppings at each other. Luke had joined them in the booth, eager to put his cooking skills to the test, only to be disappointed by the pre-determined recipes.

"Come on, guys, if you keep this up there will be nothing left for the customers," Luke watched the M&Ms soar through the air with a slight grin.

"Lighten up, Luke! We've had like four customers all day," Steven retorted, flicking some whipped cream at him. "Besides, I've got Mr. Greenburg's right here ready to go," with a wicked grin, Steven carefully placed a few jalapenos from his own lunch into the unsuspecting teacher's cookies-and-cream Beaver Tail. He couldn't help but snicker as Luke handed the teacher the treat.

"Alright, alright," Jordan conceded, handing Luke a paper towel for the whipped cream on his shirt. "I promise I will take this volunteer position more seriously, only because…"

"Son of a," Mr. Greenburg's voice rang out, the boys turned to watch the man's face turn beat red as he desperately clawed at the cap of his water bottle.

Jordan and Luke turned to look at Steven "What?" Steven asked, trying to hide the smile creeping across his face.

—-

As Rodney and Derek enjoyed their maple toffee on a stick, they stumbled upon Ally, her cheeks flushed from the cold, concentrating on a ring toss game. Despite her best efforts, the rings refused to cooperate, slipping off the bottles time after time.

"Hey, Ally," Rodney called out, catching her attention. "How are you doing?"

"I am fine," Ally said, pulling her attention away from the game. "Just was hoping to win one of these little bears." She gestured to the array of cheap colourful bears.

"You know, there's an easier way to win that teddy bear," Rodney said.

"Really?" Ally asked, fixing her purple scarf so it hung just right. "What is it?"

"Well, you need two people for it, mind if I show you?" Rodney offered, turning to Derek. "Do you mind if I help Ally out?"

"Sure thing, buddy," Derek replied, giving Rodney a knowing smile as he wandered off.

Rodney led Ally to a booth where contestants competed to fill a balloon with water using squirt guns. The first person to make their balloon burst would win a prize. Rodney explained his plan, "Since we are the only two here, it means one of us is guaranteed a prize,"

"Oh Rodney, that is genius," Ally smiled, she was excited to get the bear for her sick boyfriend, but she also chastised herself for not thinking of this on her own.

—-

Derek approached the Beaver Tail booth to throw out the stick from his toffee, spotting Steven manning the cash register. "So, they've got you handling the money, huh? I don't see anything other than a cash box back there, do they at least give you a calculator?"

"I don't need one, I can do the math quick enough in my head," Steven replied without missing a beat, a hint of pride in his voice.

"Is that so?" Derek challenged playfully. "How about we make a bet? If you can answer all my questions correctly, I'll give you a twenty-dollar tip. But if you can't, I get a free beaver tail. Deal?"

"Deal," Steven agreed, unfazed by the challenge.

Derek started with a simple question: "What's 1256 times 54?"

"67,824," Steven replied almost instantly, impressing Derek.

"Alright, what's the hypotenuse of a triangle with one side measuring 34 and the other 60?"

"68.96," Steven answered without hesitation.

"Wow, you're good," Derek admitted, raising his eyebrows. "Okay, last one: solve for x in this equation: $10x + 12 - 20 = 34x$."

Steven's brow furrowed in concentration as he began to work out the problem in his head. Just as he was about to answer, a sudden commotion erupted behind him—Jordan had accidentally caused a small oil fire and panicked while Luke smothered it. Distracted, Steven blurted out his answer: "x equals -1/6," before heading back to help put out the fire.

"Ah, so close!" Derek exclaimed when Steven returned. "It's actually x equals 1/6. I guess that means I get a free beaver tail."

"That was the deal" Steven agreed, taking Derek's order and relaying it to Jordan in the back. With his back turned Derek slipped the twenty into the small tip cup.

—-

Rodney steadied his aim, the chilled water from the squirt gun seeping into his gloves. He glanced at Ally, who was determinedly focused on her target. Distracted by how beautiful Ally looked in her lavender coat and matching toque, Rodney's aim began to falter.

Ally's balloon expanded rapidly. Within moments, it burst with a satisfying pop, showering them both with droplets of cold water.

"Congratulations! You won!" the attendant exclaimed, handing Ally the huge teddy bear she had been eyeing.

"Thanks, Rodney," Ally said with a grateful smile. "I couldn't have done it without your help."

"It was nothing," Rodney replied modestly, but Ally shook her head.

"No, really, you're special, Rodney. Sometimes I feel so dumb, like if I didn't have my looks or my athleticism, no one would want anything to do with me."

Rodney never knew she felt that way; Ally had always seemed so confident and self-assured.

"Ally, you're not dumb," Rodney reassured her. "You connect with people in a way I could never dream of. Look how quickly you made friends when you moved here, it took me twice as long just to get even one friend."

"I think you sell yourself short sometimes Rodney, but thank you," she whispered, squeezing the bear.

"Hey, you don't have to thank me. I'm just telling the truth." Rodney spotted Derek in the distance, enjoying a beaver tail. "Come on, let's go over there. You should actually meet the friend I made."

"Sure thing," she agreed, clutching the teddy bear tightly as they walked toward Derek.

"Hey, Derek!" Rodney called out as he and Ally approached the table where Derek sat, munching on a beaver tail. The scent of cinnamon and sugar drifted through the air, making Rodney's stomach growl.

"Rodney! And the famous Ally," Derek said with a warm smile, extending his hand. "I think the last time we talked was at Rodney's party."

"Oh, right," Ally replied, shaking his hand firmly. "You're a big fan of horror movies, and you hated the latest Halloween installment as much as I did."

"Ugh, don't even get me started," Derek groaned, rolling his eyes. As they launched into a spirited discussion about the movie's many flaws, Rodney felt a swell of pride that his friend and crush were getting along so well.

While Ally and Derek debated the creative choice of Michael not being the main killer, Rodney's gaze wandered across the carnival grounds. He spotted Parker and Madison sharing some taffy, both locked in conversation. He couldn't help but feel a knot in his stomach as Parker caught his eye and offered him a half-hearted grin. Rodney gave a nod in return and quickly averted his gaze.

"Hey, Rodney what do you say?" Ally asked, interrupting Rodney's thoughts.

"I'm sorry, I kind of zoned out," Rodney admitted sheepishly.

"What do you say we try the snow sculpture contest?" Ally repeated.

"Sounds fun!" Derek agreed enthusiastically, jumping to his feet.

As they made their way to the area, Rodney couldn't shake the image of

Parker's smile from his mind. Another knot slowly formed in his stomach as he wondered why Parker chose to go out with Madison in the first place. When it was his turn to tackle the mound of snow, Rodney's thoughts continued to drift back to Parker, causing him to knock the head off his sculpture and leaving him with a headless angel.

"Better luck next time, buddy," Derek chuckled as he and Ally gleefully dumped a bucket of snow onto Rodney's head. Shivering, Rodney quickly formed a snowball and returned fire.

—-

Later, as the carnival wound down, Luke, Steven, and Jordan packed up the booth. "Thanks for helping today," Jordan said with a smile. "Sorry about the whole fire thing…"

"Are you kidding?" Luke responded, sincerity in his voice. "I had a blast just hanging out!"

"Me too," Steven agreed.

With a wave, Luke left when his mom arrived to pick him up. Steven lingered for a moment before turning to leave as well. But just as he was about to go, he leaned in and planted a soft kiss on Jordan's cheek. Then, without a word, he walked away.

Jordan stood there, stunned, as Rodney and Derek approached. Unable to contain their curiosity, Jordan blurted out, "What does it mean when someone kisses you on the cheek?"

"Maybe it's just a European thing," Derek joked, but Rodney offered a more sincere answer.

"Or, it could mean they like you," he said thoughtfully.

Jordan bit their lip, eyes flickering in the direction Steven had gone. "You think so?" They wondered aloud, hope and uncertainty mingling in their voice as a small smile tugged on the corners of their mouth.

13

Do!

The sun streamed through the hallway windows, casting a blinding light on the lockers as Rodney listened to Ally's laughter. It was a sound he had come to cherish, and lately, it seemed like she was always around him. Even though she was still dating Matt, Rodney found that he could tolerate the guy for now, especially if it meant more time with Ally.

"Hey, check this out," Ally said, pulling her phone from her pocket as they stood by their lockers. She tapped on the screen, bringing up a TikTok video of a man handing out winter hats to homeless people. "I just love the giving nature of some people, you know?"

Rodney nodded, his eyes fixed on Ally's smiling face. He couldn't help but think that if he could do something similarly generous, maybe he could reignite the feelings she had for him. But what could he do? The seed of an idea began to take root in his mind – a charity event big enough to get Ally to really see him.

At lunch, Rodney sat with Derek, his tall, lean figure hunched over a tray of cafeteria tacos. Rodney picked at his own soggy taco, his thoughts consumed by the potential charity event.

"Hey, so I've been thinking," Rodney began hesitantly, "about doing something for charity. You know, like this TikTok Ally showed me earlier where they were handing out hats to the homeless."

Derek looked up from his dissection of the beef tacos, curiosity piqued.

"Oh yeah? What kind of charity thing were you thinking?"

Rodney shrugged, his brow furrowed in thought. "I don't know yet. That's why I wanted to talk to you. Maybe we can brainstorm some ideas together? After all, this could be what wins Ally over,"

"Sure thing, buddy." Derek leaned back in his chair, crossing his arms. "How about a clothing drive? People always have clothes they don't need anymore."

Rodney wrinkled his nose. "That's too basic. I want to do something different. Something that'll really make an impact."

"Okay, okay." Derek tapped his chin thoughtfully. "What about a raffle fundraiser? People love those."

Rodney's face fell. "Neither of us have anything worth raffling off, though."

Derek laughed, throwing out a series of increasingly ludicrous charity ideas – a dance-a-thon on stilts, a bake sale with only one giant cookie, a dog fashion show. Rodney laughed along with his friend, but deep down, he knew none of these ideas would win Ally over.

"Wait," Rodney said, suddenly struck by the memory of Ally going on and on about how she loved being a camp counsellor in grade 7. "What if we raised money to send kids to camp over spring break?"

Derek's eyes lit up. "That's actually a great idea! It's unique, and who can say no to helping kids, you would have to be heartless. Ally would definitely be impressed."

Derek's words filled Rodney with a warm sense of hopefulness. How hard could it be to set up a charity, anyway?

—-

Rodney could feel the bead of sweat drip down his back as he stood outside the principal's office, clutching a folder filled with his charity proposal. Taking a deep breath, he knocked on the door and heard the muffled invitation to come in.

"Ah, Rodney, what can I do for you?" Principal Jenkins asked, peering at him over the rims of her glasses.

"I have an idea for a charity event, ma'am," Rodney said, opening the folder and presenting it to her. "It's called 'Camp for Kids.' We want to raise money to send kids to camp over spring break."

As Principal Jenkins leafed through the paperwork, her eyes sparkled with interest. "This is an excellent idea, Rodney. I'm impressed." She handed the folder back to him. "I'll support this initiative. You'll be responsible for making announcements, gathering volunteers, and collecting funds."

"Thank you so much, ma'am!" Rodney beamed, feeling a surge of pride.

However, as he left the principal's office, the weight of responsibility began to sink in. There was so much to do, and he wasn't sure where to start. All he had was an agreement with the school board to distribute all funds raised to the families that needed them. He felt his chest tighten, and his vision blurred as panic threatened to take hold. Desperate for guidance, he found himself in Mr. Rogo's office.

"Mr. Rogo, I need your help," Rodney blurted out, his voice tight with stress. "I've started this charity, but there's so much work, and I don't know how to handle it all. I don't know why I thought I could do this."

"Take a deep breath, Rodney," Mr. Rogo said calmly, motioning for him to sit. "First things first, have you asked your friends for help."

"Not really, honestly things have been going great with my friends and all," Rodney sighed, rubbing his temples. "But I feel like I would be taking advantage of them if I asked them to help."

"Rodney, you are not taking advantage of them by asking for their help, helping is what friends do for each other," Mr. Rogo explained, a gentle smile on his face. "Give it a try."

Feeling a little more hopeful, Rodney pulled out his phone and sent a group message to Ally, Parker, Jordan, Madison, and Derek, explaining the charity idea and asking for their assistance.

"Hey guys, I'm working on a charity called Camp for Kids," he typed, his fingers flying across the screen. "We're raising money to send kids to camp over spring break. Would any of you like to help?"

Derek's response was almost immediate: "I thought I was already the CEO of this, lol!"

Rodney's heart soared at Derek's support, but he couldn't help feeling disappointed as the hours ticked by without any other replies. The next day, however, Jordan sent him a message: "I'd be happy to help, Rodney! This sounds like a great cause."

"Thanks, Jordan. It means a lot," Rodney replied, relief washing over him. At least he didn't have to do it on his own, and it could be fun since Jordan was so easygoing. But the lack of response from Ally was troubling, after all, she was totally into this kind of thing.

Rodney shook his head, trying not to dwell on the lack of response. He had a charity to run, after all, and he was sure once it took off Ally would notice.

—-

The next day at school, Jordan's artistic talents were on full display as they meticulously crafted vibrant posters for the charity. Rodney watched in awe as splashes of colour and realistic scenery came to life under Jordan's skilled hands. Each poster depicted happy kids at different camps with slogans like "Send a Kid to Camp, Change a Life" and "Camp for Kids: Making Dreams Come True."

"Wow, Jordan, these are amazing," Rodney gushed, as he picked up one of the posters.

"Thanks," Jordan replied with a grin. "I just hope they'll catch people's attention and help us raise some money."

Meanwhile, Derek had taken it upon himself to go on the morning announcements every day that week, spreading the word about Camp for Kids and urging students to bring money to their homeroom teachers. Though he spoke with enthusiasm and conviction, what really helped was by all accounts Derek was a good-looking guy.

Rodney did his part by delivering forms to each homeroom teacher, ensuring they knew how to track the funds collected and who the donations were from. As he went from classroom to classroom, he couldn't help but feel a sense of pride swelling within him. What started out as a way to impress Ally had turned into something he was actually proud of.

"Here you go, Ms. Jenkins," Rodney said, handing over a stack of forms. "And if you have any questions, just let me know."

"Thank you, Rodney," she replied with a warm smile. "This is such a wonderful cause. I'm sure we'll be able to raise a lot of money."

But at the end of the week, when they tallied up the donations, the boys were disappointed to discover they had only raised a meagre two hundred dollars. Frustration bubbled inside Rodney as he stared at the pitiful amount. It wasn't even enough to send two kids to camp.

"Maybe we should ask Parker for help again," Rodney suggested, knowing they needed all the assistance they could get. But when he approached his friend, Parker just shook his head.

"Sorry, man," Parker said apologetically. "Between my family, my job, and schoolwork, I barely have enough time to do the things I want to do."

Feeling a twinge of betrayal, Rodney turned to Madison, who was standing nearby. "What about you? Would you be willing to help?"

"Uh, no thanks," she replied dismissively, flipping her hair over her shoulder. "I don't think it will look good on a college app to be a part of a failed charity, you understand." Rodney rolled his eyes and walked away feeling defeated.

As Rodney walked home with Derek that day, he couldn't contain his frustrations any longer. "It's so hard to get the money we need when no one else seems to want to pitch in!" he ranted. "We're trying our best, but it's not enough. Maybe we should be talking to the parents. They're the ones with the money, after all."

Derek mulled over the idea, nodding thoughtfully. "You know what? You might be onto something there. Call Jordan and see if they can come over tonight."

"OK," Rodney agreed, unsure of what Derek had in mind. "Are you going to fill me in on the plan here?"

"You said it yourself, we need to get the message out to the parents," Derek said, clapping Rodney on the back. "All it takes is a guilt trip in the form of a letter and parents line up to shell out."

—-

Later that evening, Rodney, Derek, and Jordan huddled around the dining table at Derek's house, brainstorming ideas for their letter to the parents. The room was bathed in a warm, golden glow from the overhead chandelier, as the boys attempted to write the letter.

"Dear esteemed guardians," Rodney began, his pen hovering over the paper as he furrowed his brow. "We humbly beseech you to consider the importance of—"

"Whoa there, Shakespeare," Derek interrupted, grinning. "You're trying way too hard. We need something that'll grab their attention. Like, THINK OF THE CHILDREN!" he laughed.

Jordan fidgeted nervously with their sleeves, eyes darting between Rodney and Derek. "I-I don't know how to help," they admitted, their voice barely above a whisper. "I hate writing letters,"

Derek leaned back in his chair, tapping his chin thoughtfully. "What if we just make up reasons why kids should go to camp over spring break? The real reasons, like having fun and being safe, are boring. We need something catchy."

Rodney seemed a little worried by the suggestion. "What do mean? Are you saying we lie and say things like 'Not sending your kids to camp will make them so lazy they will never get a job.'"

"Close but that is not quite scary enough to really get the money flowing," Derek responded.

"I wasn't being serious,"

"Oh, you are thinking more like without camp your child will start drinking and smoking out of boredom!" Jordan proposed, sounding uncertain about their suggestion.

Derek's smile broadened as he started typing away on his laptop. "And all that drinking and smoking will turn them into vandals and arsonists!"

"Ha! Don't forget murderers!" Jordan added, laughing.

"Right," Rodney said, finally conceding to the fun the other two seemed to be having. "And they'll spend their lives in and out of prison."

The three friends shared a good laugh over their fake letter, their earlier frustrations momentarily forgotten. "Okay," Rodney said, wiping tears from his eyes. "Let's get serious and work on the real letter now."

"Tomorrow," Derek agreed, still chuckling. "I am afraid I have to kick you out, parents have a strict no-one here past ten policy."

Jordan and Rodney left Derek's house, feeling lighter, despite the fact they hadn't actually written a letter to the parents they could use.

——

The following Monday, Rodney's heart dropped when his teacher handed him a letter to take home to his parents. The familiar lines of their joke letter stared back at him, sending a shiver down his spine. Panicked, he rushed to find Derek, clutching their apparent joke letter.

"Derek! Why did you choose to send our joke home with the entire student body?!" Rodney demanded, his voice cracking.

"Relax, man," Derek said calmly, resting a hand on Rodney's shoulder. "I thought about it a lot and this letter is going to do exactly what we need it to do. Money for the kids and a successful charity that Ally won't be able to ignore, it's a win-win"

Rodney hesitated, torn between anger and trust. He knew Derek only wanted to help, and it was too late to take back all the letters anyway. With a deep breath, he nodded, hoping against hope that this gamble would pay off.

14

I

The school hallways buzzed as students handed over crumpled bills and envelopes filled with cheques, all destined for the Camps for Kids charity. Rodney stood in front of a large cardboard box, watching as it slowly filled with generous donations. Derek leaned against the wall nearby, arms crossed, an impressed smile on his face.

"Looks like our little note did the trick," he said, nodding towards the growing pile of money.

"Definitely," Rodney agreed, nervously. "But now we've got a different problem on our hands. We need more help to gather and count all these donations."

Jordan overheard the conversation and chimed in. "I know someone who'd be perfect for this. I'll go ask Steven if he wants to help out."

Rodney watched as Jordan walked confidently down the hallway, their paisley-patterned pants drawing the attention of a group of girls walking by. They approached Steven, who stood by his locker, fiddling with the combination lock. As Jordan spoke to him, Rodney could have sworn he saw Steven blushing, and he nodded vigorously in agreement.

"Welcome to the team, Steven," Rodney said as Jordan led him back to the group.

"Thanks, guys," Steven replied, his voice wavering slightly. He glanced at Jordan, trying his best to look cool and collected. "I'm really excited to help out."

"This is going to be great," Jordan explained, "Steven is like a math genius, he'll be able to count it faster than all of us combine." Derek nodded in agreement.

"I mean I am ok with numbers." Steven tried to downplay it, not wanting to embarrass himself if he messed up.

"Great," Rodney said, giving Steven a reassuring smile. "You and Jordan can start collecting donations from the homerooms. We'll regroup here to count it during lunch."

As Jordan and Steven set off down the hallway side by side, Jordan stole glances at Steven, admiring the way his hair seemed to catch the light just right. They cleared their throat nervously, gathering the courage to bring up the kiss that had been playing on a loop in their mind.

"Hey, Steven," they began hesitantly, "I've been meaning to ask… Why did you kiss me on the cheek after the winter carnival?"

Steven paused for a moment, his eyes twinkling as they recalled that afternoon. "Well, we had a lot of fun together selling beaver tails, didn't we? And I thought you were being pretty cute, so I just went for it." He offered an apologetic smile. "I'm sorry if I crossed a line or anything."

"No, no," Jordan stammered, feeling the heat rise to their cheeks. "I actually, um, liked it. A lot. And I was wondering if maybe… you'd like to go out sometime?"

"Really?" Steven's face broke into a wide grin. "I mean I have never really been on a date before, like a real date."

"Neither have I" Jordan laughed, "But I would like to stumble through one with you."

Steven's face turned beet red, "I would like that a lot." he said with a smile.

With newfound confidence, Steven and Jordan continued their mission to collect donations, stealing glances at each other as they went.

———-

Rodney stood in the hallway, absent-mindedly fidgeting with his backpack strap as he and Derek collected the envelopes from homerooms.

"Man, we really need more hands on deck," Derek commented, scratching the back of his head. "Why don't you try asking Ally for help again?"

"Ally?" Rodney hesitated, remembering how she had completely ignored the text the first time around and had been acting like she never actually got it. "I'm not sure that's a good idea. Maybe we should ask Parker again? They say the third time is the charm."

"Come on, Rodney," Derek urged. "Wasn't the reason for starting all this to impress her? And you never know maybe she actually didn't get the message."

With a reluctant sigh, Rodney agreed. "Alright, I'll give it a shot."

After school, Rodney found Ally by her locker, chatting animatedly with a group of fellow yoga club members. The sight of her leaning against the row of lockers made his heart race, and he swallowed hard before approaching her.

"Hey, Ally," he said, trying to sound casual. "Can I talk to you for a second?"

"Sure, what's up?" Ally replied, her eyes shining with curiosity as she stepped away from her friends.

"Uh, well, the charity I started has actually taken off, and we need some extra help." Rodney rubbed the back of his neck, feeling exposed under her gaze. "Would you be interested in joining us?"

Ally's expression flickered, and she seemed to be searching for the right words. "I, um, don't think I can," she stammered, her cheeks flushing pink.

"Oh, OK," Rodney said, he wanted to turn and leave but he needed to know why. After all, he thought they had made real progress in being friends again. "Can I ask why? I mean if it is like a time thing I can make sure that you don't have to do too much, maybe just collect donations in the morning. There is only a week left."

She sighed, her eyes downcast. "It's Matt," she admitted. "He is really making progress and trying to be supportive in his own Matt way, but his parents are going through a thing and he kind of just feels really insecure in our relationship right now and I don't want to make it worse."

Rodney's heart sank, but he couldn't fault her loyalty. "Oh, I'm sorry. I just thought we were ok, I mean we have been hanging out more and stuff."

"We are ok Rodney, but I don't want to push it. Especially with all the stuff from earlier" Ally whispered, her voice heavy with regret. "I'm sorry." She scooped her backpack off the ground and retreated back into her friends.

As Rodney walked away, his mind went into overdrive. It felt like they were falling back into the old pattern – and he didn't want to back to feeling like hanging out with Ally was an impossibility. But how could he convince her to join them without jeopardizing her relationship with Matt?

"Sorry" wasn't going to be enough to deter Rodney from trying again. He wanted to spend more time with her and Matt wasn't going to stop him. He just had to find a way to make sure Matt wouldn't get too jealous.

"Wait!" Rodney called out, his voice cracking as Ally and her group started heading for the stairs. She stopped, turning back to look at him with a puzzled expression. He knew he had to act fast, so he blurted out the first thing that came to mind. "I have a girlfriend, so Matt doesn't need to worry about us hanging out, it is strictly as friends after all."

Ally's eyebrows rose in surprise, her blue eyes studying him closely. "Really? I haven't seen you hanging around any girls lately."

Rodney felt the heat rise to his cheeks, but he couldn't back down now. "Well, we're keeping it casual and haven't labelled it yet," he lied, hoping she would buy it.

She tilted her head and considered this for a moment. "So we would just be working together and Matt wouldn't have a reason to feel nervous," she said slowly as if piecing together a puzzle. "Who is the mystery girl?"

He hesitated, feeling a knot form in his stomach. "Oh uh, well I said I wouldn't tell anyone about us until she was ready," he admitted, careful not to confirm it outright. Something in Ally's face shifted, and Rodney held his breath, waiting for her response.

"Alright then," she said finally, her demeanour warming. "If that's the case, I'll help out with the charity." Relief washed over Rodney, and he tried to hide his grin. Ally pulled out her phone and quickly sent a message to Matt, "OK, we should be good to go."

"Great! Let's meet up at my house, I still have some money that needs counting and could use the help if you have time?" Rodney suggested, trying to sound as he watched Ally's friends eyeing him over her shoulder.

"Sure, I can swing that," Ally replied, with a smile that made Rodney want to melt. She returned to her friends and Rodney felt like he won the lottery.

As they sorted through the piles of donations that night, Ally glanced over to Rodney. "You know, we should all go on a double date sometime. I want to meet the girl who won you over," she proposed, clearly eager to get to know Rodney's supposed girlfriend.

Rodney felt his heart race and a bead of sweat trickle down his temple. He hated that he lied to her, but admitting the truth would surely ruin his chances of hanging out with Ally. So, he swallowed hard and nodded. "That sounds like fun," he agreed, trying to sound enthusiastic while secretly dreading the thought.

"Perfect! Let's plan for this Friday," Ally said with a grin, as she tore open an envelope. Rodney forced a smile, but on the inside, it felt like someone lit him on fire. By this weekend Ally would know he lied to her, and their friendship would ruined.

———-

The school corridor seemed unusually dark the next day as if the fluorescent lights were mocking Rodney's predicament. He spotted Derek leaning against a row of lockers and hurried over. He needed a plan and fast.

"Hey, Derek, I really need to talk to you," Rodney whispered, his eyes darting around nervously.

"Whoa, slow down there, buddy," Derek replied, taking in Rodney's clearly frantic state. "What happened?"

"Okay, so… I lied to Ally about having a girlfriend so she'd join our charity, and we could hang out together. And then she suggested a double date this Friday with her and Matt, and I agreed to it!" Rodney explained in a single breath, his voice cracking at the end.

Derek raised an eyebrow, clearly amused by the situation. "You agreed to this?"

"What else was I supposed to do? I panicked," Rodney admitted, his face flushing with embarrassment. "Now what do I do?"

"Simple, just say your date is sick on Friday," Derek offered, but Rodney shook his head.

"That's a one-time excuse, Derek. What if they want to reschedule? If

Ally finds out I lied, forget dating, she will never want to see my face again!" Rodney countered, his anxiety creeping back in.

"Alright, then let's find you a fake girlfriend," Derek suggested as if it were the most obvious solution. "Someone who'll pretend to go out with you."

"Who would ever do that?" Rodney asked skeptically.

"Ask Erica," Derek offered. "You guys are friends, right?"

Rodney hesitated, recalling how he left Parker behind to meet Erica. He always felt unease around her, like she was always analyzing his every move. "I guess, but we haven't really talked since I was grounded."

"Then now's the perfect time," Derek encouraged, giving Rodney a reassuring pat on the back. "Either that or tell Ally the truth and accept the consequences."

"Alright," Rodney didn't want to do it but what other choice did he have?

Later that day, after gym class, Rodney caught up with Erica in the hallway. Her light brown hair framed her face in loose waves, and she was taking a drink from the fountain. Rodney could feel himself sweating as he approached her.

"Hey, Erica," he said, inching closer. "We haven't hung out in a while. Maybe we should, now that I'm not grounded anymore."

Her face lit up, and Rodney felt a wave of relief wash over him. "I'd love that! I've missed hanging out with you."

"Great!" Rodney replied, encouraged by her enthusiasm. "Actually, there's something else I wanted to ask you. I need a huge favour… Would you go on a double date with me this Friday?"

He quickly explained the situation, watching Erica's eyes widen with amusement as he recounted his lie about having a girlfriend. To his surprise, she agreed without hesitation.

"Sounds fun! I am always down for a free meal," she said, grinning.

"Thank you so much, Erica. You're a lifesaver," Rodney sighed, feeling a weight lifted off his shoulders.

———-

The next day, Rodney met Erica before the bell rang. He knew that he and Erica had to sell their fake relationship convincingly, or his lie would crumble around him.

"Ready for our debut?" she whispered, a playful smirk gracing her lips.

"Ready as I'll ever be," Rodney replied, taking a deep breath as they approached Ally and Matt. The two stood by a row of lockers, completely engrossed in each other's company, making it all too easy for Rodney and Erica to saunter past them.

"Hey Ally," Rodney called out casually, catching her attention. "Hey Matt."

"Hey guys," Ally responded, her eyes flickering between Rodney and Erica's intertwined hands. She nudged Matt with her elbow, nodding towards the couple. "See? I told you nothing is going on, Rodney is dating someone and is happy."

Matt, however, looked unconvinced as he appraised the pair. "Who'd want to go out with Rodney after all the weird stuff he's done this year?"

"Matt!" Ally scolded, her cheeks flushing as she gave him a small punch to the arm. "I wish you wouldn't talk about my friend like that."

"Relax, babe," Matt replied, attempting to placate her with a charming smile. "I'm just saying they already gave it a shot and it didn't work, why would they try again."

"I don't know, but you should change your attitude before our double date," Ally warned, clearly unhappy with his behaviour.

As Erica and Rodney continued down the hall, Parker and Madison caught sight of Erica and Rodney holding hands. Madison beamed with pride, eager to take credit for their union. "I set those two up, you know. My matchmaking skills have always been on the mark."

"Really?" Parker asked skeptically, raising an eyebrow. "I don't know if I buy it. They're so different. Rodney's weird in a good way, with all these layers to who he is as a person. Erica has a YouTube channel devoted to different shades of eyeliner."

"Are you jealous?" Madison teased, giving him a playful nudge. "If I didn't know better, I'd think you were into Rodney."

"Of course not," Parker scoffed, his cheeks reddening slightly. "I'm just looking out for my friends."

"Uh-huh, sure," Madison said, grinning. She leaned in and pressed her lips against Parker's to halt the conversation, leaving him momentarily breathless. "I am just teasing you, babe," she said as she pulled away. She headed to class and Parker stared at the spot where Rodney once stood.

97

15

Just

Rodney swallowed hard standing outside the restaurant, he didn't think Ally would have chosen such a high-end place for a double date. Under the dim, elegant lights of The Clock Tower, Rodney nervously adjusted his emerald green bow tie, the fabric matching Erica's stunning dress. As they entered the restaurant, the clinking of glasses and soft murmurs of conversation filled the air. Matt and Ally were already waiting at their reserved table, and the moment Rodney saw them he realized just how overdressed they were.

"Hey, guys," Rodney greeted them, feeling a flutter of nerves in his stomach. He took Erica's coat for her and hung it on the back of her chair, earning her an appreciative smile. Ally watched the exchange with envy, glancing at Matt who was pretending to read the menu.

"Artichoke dip sounds good, right?" Rodney asked as they settled into their seats, and he glanced over the menu. Everyone murmured in agreement, and he ordered the appetizer for the table.

Matt, still eyeing Rodney skeptically, leaned forward. "So, how did you two lovebirds end up back together again?" He grinned, hoping to catch Rodney in a lie.

Erica gave a warm laugh, her eyes twinkling. "It was actually really sweet. I dropped my science project in the hallway - a DNA strand made of pipe cleaners - and Rodney helped me reconstruct it right there on the spot." She leaned over and pressed a tender kiss to Rodney's cheek, causing Matt's grin to falter. "He is just the most kind-hearted person I know and I knew I had to give him another chance." Matt rolled his eyes, seeming almost disgusted by this answer.

The server returned ready to take their orders, Matt ordered a salad for Ally, while Erica and Rodney decided to share a massive stack of nachos. Rodney could sense the tension growing between Matt and Ally and tried to steer the conversation away from anything that could cause conflict.

"Remember that time back in Toronto when we played at that elementary school playground close to the lake?" Rodney asked Ally, he had noticed she had been oddly quiet so far. "These older kids stole my bike, and you chased them down. You threw a stick through the spokes!"

Ally laughed, her cheek flushed a shade of pink. "That kid ate dirt! I was pretty badass, wasn't I?"

"Definitely," Rodney agreed, happy to see Ally joining the conversation.

Matt's annoyance bubbled over as he noticed Ally seemed to be almost glowing as she recounted more stories from Toronto with Rodney. He couldn't stand the fact that everyone seemed to be buying Rodney's innocent act except for him. He slid his arm around Ally, trying to assert his desirability. "Well, if we're talking about impressive feats, two nights ago I single-handedly won the Rockets game for us. We were down by 3 but I scored a hat trick in under a minute."

Erica attempted to join in "Oh no way, my hockey team had a pretty close game recently too," but Matt cut her off with a dismissive wave of his hand. Inside, Rodney winced at Matt's behaviour. All he'd wanted was to work with Ally on the charity, but the result of his lie was this dinner and Matt seemed about to pop. But he played along, masking his concern with a smile, hoping it would all work out in the end.

Ally's patience however had reached its breaking point; she could no longer ignore Matt's behaviour. "I need to go," she declared, pushing back her chair and standing up. "I'm going home." She turned to Rodney and Erica, an apologetic smile on her lips. "I'm sorry, you guys but I am just not feeling well. I hope you understand,"

"Ally, wait!" Matt called out, not seeming to realize the last thing she wanted right now was to talk to him. He scrambled after her, leaving Rodney and Erica alone at the table.

"Ally, are you mad at me?" Matt asked as he caught up with her outside. "Because I am sorry, but Rodney just gets under my skin. Like, it is so clear he wants you and this dinner has to be some kind of scheme. I just don't know what it is yet."

"Matt, it's clear you're jealous of my friendship with him. You need to fix it if you want us to stay together. This isn't a scheme, this is Rodney. Erica was right, he is the kindest person I know." Ally replied, her voice firm but laced with disappointment. She didn't wait for a response, walking away into the night.

——-

Back inside the restaurant, Rodney rubbed his temples, worry etched on his face. "We might've just ruined Ally's relationship," he muttered. "I feel bad about it."

Erica leaned in, a wicked glint in her eyes. "But wasn't that the goal?"

"No! I mean yes, I don't know. It feels so wrong," Rodney suggested, holding his stomach as if it were aching.

"Wow, you really are too sweet Rodney," Erica laughed, " It was pretty clear to me those two were never going to last anyway. I say if she doesn't see what a catch you are, she doesn't deserve you. Why not give something new a try," She traced the rim of her wine glass seductively.

"Oh, uh, I don't think I am ready for anything new right now." Rodney's words were gentle, but firm.

"Of course," Erica replied, the corners of her mouth twitching with feigned indifference. Rodney settled the bill, each lost in his own thoughts.

——-

Monday morning found Rodney and Ally counting the money raised for their charity over the past week. He wasn't sure if he should bring up the weirdness of Friday's double date or just pretend like it never happened.

"Rodney, I'm sorry about Matt," she said, breaking the silence. "I just wish he'd stop trying to be better than everyone else and be himself."

"Being yourself can be scary," Rodney replied, taking the seat next to her.

"Sometimes, I don't even know who I am."

"Rodney, you've always been you, and that's what I admire about you. It's why Erica likes you so much." Ally offered a reassuring smile.

"Actually, Erica and I broke up over the weekend." Rodney focused intently on counting the money, avoiding eye contact.

"Oh Rodney, I'm sorry. But you'll find someone in no time," Ally assured him, moving to hug him before deciding against it.

"Maybe, but I think I just want to focus on the charity for now." He glanced up at her, gauging her reaction.

Ally raised an eyebrow as if she were shocked anyone would be happy without a partner. "Well, alright then. Let's get back to work, shall we."

As they sorted through the piles of cash and coins, their conversation shifted to the upcoming spring break, the shadow of Friday night's events gradually fading into memory.

———-

Madison leaned against her locker, watching as Parker approached with a spring in his step. She took a deep breath, inhaling the familiar scent of textbooks and pencil shavings that filled the hallway.

"Hey," she said, her voice hesitant. "Did you hear about Erica and Rodney breaking up again?"

"Oh? Did they?" Parker feigned surprise, but the corners of his mouth tugged into a subtle smile. "Well, I guess I was right about them after all."

"Wait, why are you smiling?" Madison's brow furrowed as she wondered why his friend's heartbreak would make him so happy.

"Smiling? Me?" Parker quickly wiped the expression off his face, trying to play it off. "I'm not smiling. Anyway, I should go check on Rodney to see how he's doing." He turned to leave as Madison crossed her arms as she thought.

Parker had seemed against Erica and Rodney from the beginning, but why? Her fingers tapped anxiously on her phone, as she tried to figure out why Parker was acting so weird. A flurry of texts flew between her and Erica, revealing a long-forgotten history of hand-holding in middle school.

Later that day, Madison confronted Parker beneath the shadow of a towering oak tree by the soccer fields, its buds just beginning to open.

"Ever since we got together," she began, her voice wavering, "I feel like I've been putting in more effort than you have in our relationship. It's like you love someone else, but you're just not being upfront about it." She hoped he would reassure her that she was wrong.

Parker's gaze dropped to the ground, his hands fidgeting with the hem of his jacket. "Look, I do have feelings for someone else. I can't seem to get over them, no matter how hard I try."

Madison's heart sank. "It's Erica, isn't it?" Her voice cracked with emotion as she continued, "I know about how you two had a thing in middle school. I don't want to be the girl you settle for, Parker."

"No, Madison, it's not-" But before Parker could clarify, she had already stormed off, tears streaming down her cheeks. He watched her go, breathing a small sigh of relief.

———-

The sleek, modern interior of Sushi Galore in London felt worlds away from the familiar, casual hangouts Jordan and Steven frequented back in Strathroy. A crystal chandelier hung above their table, casting glimmers of light that danced across Jordan's dyed hair like tiny stars.

"Wow, this place is… fancy," Jordan commented, a hint of concern creeping into their voice as they took in the immaculate white tablecloth and chopsticks.

"Uh, yeah. I just looked for the highest-rated sushi place," Steven replied, his fingers nervously gripping the menu, as he adjusted his watch. "This is apparently the best there is."

"It's certainly priced that way," Jordan joked, trying to put Steven at ease. "The fish tank is nice, I like the blue tang they have." Steven nodded and the two fell silent.

As they perused the menu and ordered their dishes, they remained in total silence, a far cry from the effortless banter they usually shared. Steven's gaze darted around the room, avoiding eye contact, and Jordan couldn't help but notice just how off he was.

"Steven, this is weird right?" Jordan finally asked, unable to take the tension any longer. "Like why has this felt so hard."

"I know…" Steven hesitated for a moment, "I've never dated another guy… sorry non-binary person before."

Jordan laughed, knowing this was the first time Steven had taken anyone on a date. They leaned in closer, offering a reassuring smile. "I am aware, remember we are in the same boat here. You don't have to go out of your way to impress me, I already really like you."

"Right, of course." Relief washed over Steven's face, but it was quickly followed by a tinge of regret. "I still feel like I messed up this date, though."

"Hey, it's okay." Jordan laughed as another round of rolls arrived. "Maybe next time we can go somewhere more our speed?"

"Deal," Steven agreed, a genuine smile slowly spreading across his face.

———-

The following day, as students ate the usual from the cafeteria, Steven approached Jordan's table with a tray of McDonald's in hand. "Thought this might be more our style."

"Definitely!" Jordan grinned, eagerly unwrapping a cheeseburger. "This beats raw fish any day!" They shared a laugh and began to dig into their meal.

As they finished lunch, Steven leaned in, gently brushing his lips against Jordan's. Their first public kiss felt like a promise, a declaration of commitment. They pulled away, cheeks flushed and hearts racing.

"Jordan," Steven said, his voice filled with sincerity, "I really like you."

"Steven, I really like you too," Jordan replied, their eyes meeting with warmth and understanding.

16

Want

The eager chatter of students filled the crowded school hallway, accompanied by the faint scent of excitement and anticipation. Lockers slammed and locks clicked, as they shared plans for the much-awaited spring break. Rodney trailed along beside Derek, who animatedly described his upcoming Bahamas fishing adventure with his older brother.

"Seriously, Rodney, you should see my brother's girlfriend." Derek shook his head in disbelief, his eyes wide. "She's a total smoke show. I don't get what she sees in him."

Rodney couldn't help but smile at Derek's description, but his thoughts quickly drifted back to his own lack of plans for the break. He was distracted by the notion of no one being around over the break to hang with, when they bumped into Parker. Parker's ginger curls bounced around his face as he adjusted his glasses.

"Seriously we need to stop bumping into each other like this," He laughed, looking at Rodney, "What had you so distracted?" Parker asked as he adjusted his backpack straps.

"March break plans," Derek replied, looping an arm around Parker's shoulder and pulling him into their conversation. "I'm off to the Bahamas. How about you, Parker?"

"Actually, I'll be working as a camp counsellor at Long Horn Ranch," Parker said with a touch of pride in his voice. "Gotta make some extra cash, and it's kind of like a vacation too, we get some time every day to do what we want."

"Nice!" Derek nodded approvingly. "What about you, Rodney?"

Rodney hesitated before admitting, "I won't be doing much. Just… avoiding my mom, I guess." He swallowed hard, remembering how they hadn't really talked since their fight. He wondered how a week stuck in a house together would go. "We haven't really talked since our fight. I shouldn't have brought up Dad's death like that."

Derek's eyes softened as he gave Rodney a small squeeze. "She's your mom dude, she knows you didn't mean it. It's a parent thing,"

Rodney nodded, but he couldn't shake off the guilt. "Yeah, but still don't feel good about it," he murmured, just as the bell rang, signalling the end of their conversation. The boys exchanged quick goodbyes before going their separate ways to class.

As Rodney walked away, he couldn't help but wonder if he would be able to make it right with his mom.

Rodney slid into his seat in art class, the whiff of oil paint and damp clay made him feel even more nauseous. He glanced around and found Madison and Jordan already at their easels, streaks of colour smeared across their aprons.

"Hey," he said as he squeezed a dollop of paint onto his palette.

"Hey, Rodney!" Madison greeted him with a warm smile, while Jordan offered a casual nod, their lavender-tinted hair matching the background of their portrait.

Ms. Bacon clapped her hands, drawing the class's attention. "Alright, everyone! Today, we'll be working on your self-portraits. I want you to incorporate elements from your life into your painting. It could be anything – your hobbies, loved ones, or even your dreams."

She gestured toward a canvas propped up on a nearby table. Rodney squinted, recognizing Matt's unmistakable signature – bold strokes, muted colours, and intricate detail. The portrait displayed Matt's face, but it was tinged with sadness, his eyes seeming lost. Behind him, a dense forest loomed, giving the impression that one could step right into it and become swallowed by the darkness.

"Wow, I didn't know Matt had it in him," Jordan murmured, a note of surprise in their voice.

"Me neither," Rodney agreed quietly, his thoughts drifting to Matt's home situation, he didn't know much, just that his parents were fighting. Was this painting reflecting how these fights made Matt feel, or did he feel this lost even before the fighting started?

As the trio began sketching out their portraits, Madison's voice broke the silence. "So, guess what? I got a last-minute gig as a lifeguard! With the money, I'll finally be able to afford Taylor Swift tickets."

"Damn, they must be paying you in gold if you can afford those tickets from one week of work," Jordan joked, eliciting a laugh from Madison.

"Which camp is it?" Rodney asked, curiosity piqued.

"Long Horn Ranch," Madison replied, carefully dabbing paint onto her canvas.

Rodney's heart skipped a beat – the same camp where Parker would be working. He contemplated warning her that her recent ex would be there too. But he thought there was no need to stir up drama and ruin her spring break plans.

"Sounds fun," Rodney remarked instead, forcing a smile as he dipped his brush into the paint. "I'm sure you'll have a great time."

"Thanks! I'm really looking forward to it," Madison said, her eyes sparkling with excitement.

———-

Lunchtime arrived and the fragrant scent of pizza filled the air. Rodney scanned the room, his gaze drifting from table to table until it landed on Ally, who sat alone by the window, her eyes fixed on the raindrops tracing their way down the glass.

"Hey," Rodney said as he slid into the seat across from her, balancing his tray carefully. "How are things?"

"They are fine," Ally replied, looking up from the window. "I just needed a little space today."

"Gotcha." Rodney nodded in understanding. "I can go if you want me to?"

"No, you can stay," she said without making eye contact.

"Ok," Rodney tried to think of something that may lighten the mood and cheer her up, "So, what are you doing for spring break?"

"Going back to Toronto for the week," she said, picking at the crust of her pizza. "And you?"

"Staying here mostly," Rodney admitted. "Trying to avoid my mom, I guess."

"Sorry to hear that." Ally's expression softened.

"How are things with Matt?"

"Uh, not great," she confessed, her fingers twisting the corner of her napkin. "After his latest outburst, I think some time apart might be good for us."

The thought of Ally and Matt breaking up sent a thrill through Rodney, but he forced himself to wear a sympathetic frown. "I'm really sorry, Ally. That must be tough."

"Thanks," she sighed. "It is, but I'll manage."

Just then, Steven and Jordan approached, their hands clasped together, looking somewhat nervous. "Hey, guys," Jordan began. "We wanted to tell you something."

"Go for it," Rodney encouraged, curiosity piqued.

"Steven and I… we're dating now." Jordan's cheeks flushed a soft pink. "We wanted our friends to know before we post it to the socials."

A grin spread across Ally's face as she stood up and pulled them both into a warm embrace. "Thank you for trusting us with this. I'm so happy for you!"

"Congrats," Rodney said, beaming at the new couple. As he watched their happiness, it was the first time it dawned on him that you didn't have to just date a girl if you were a guy. He thought of the way he felt around Parker, his smile, the way they always seemed to bump into each other. Could the way he had been feeling be love? For the first time, he felt like maybe they were.

"Thanks, Rodney," Steven said, giving him a polite nod.

"Really, you two are great together," Ally gushed as they all sat down to eat.

"Well sit down and tell me everything," Ally started, taking her seat. Jordan and Steven sat across from her and began the story of how it all started. As they chatted, Rodney's mind continued to wander through the possibilities of what could be. Was it possible he wanted to be with Parker more than he wanted to be with Ally?

———-

The moment Rodney stepped through the front door, he found Marcy bouncing on her toes, a grin so wide it threatened to split her face in two. Their mother stood behind her, a secretive smile playing at the corners of her lips. A knot of anticipation twisted in Rodney's gut.

"Rodney!" Marcy squealed, unable to contain herself any longer. "Mom has the most amazing news!"

"Alright," he said, trying to keep his voice steady as he looked between the two of them.

"Okay, well," their mother chimed in, her excitement bubbling over. "I managed to save up enough money this year to take us all on a trip to Disney World for March break."

"Disney World?" Rodney's eyes widened in disbelief, his heart leaping in his chest. "That's incredible!" But then, a shadow of doubt crossed his mind, had he made her feel so guilty she decided to take them on a trip? "What made you think of this?"

"Sweetheart, this was the plan since we moved here. I think it would be good for us to take a few trips together every year as a family." She gave him a reassuring smile, and Rodney felt even more guilty about everything he had said to her.

"Wow, thanks, Mom! This is amazing!" He gave her a small hug before he pulled out his phone and quickly texted Derek about the trip. Within seconds, Derek responded: 'Dude, that sounds epic! Have fun!'

Later that evening, Rodney found himself seated at the dinner table, unsure how to join in on the conversation – he had felt so terrible it was hard to speak around his family. The delicious scent of roasted chicken filled the air, mingling with the lively chatter of his mom and sister. It felt like a cozy blanket, wrapping itself around them while he was out in the cold.

As Marcy stood up to clear the dishes, she gave Rodney an encouraging nod. With his sister gone, he seized the opportunity to speak privately with their mom.

"Mom, can we talk?" he asked tentatively.

"Of course, Rodney." She looked at him with those deep, understanding eyes that he hadn't seen since his dad had passed.

"I just want to say… I'm really sorry for how things have been between us since Dad passed away," Rodney started, but she stopped him right there.

Her voice quivered slightly. "I am the one who is sorry. I've felt like a part of myself has been missing ever since that day. I lost my husband, my best friend, and my partner in life. I have been so mad about how it happened… but I never meant to take it out on you, I am so sorry."

Rodney felt his chest tighten, the weight of her words pressing down on him. He didn't know what to say; all he could do was wrap his arms around her and hold her close. Together, they let the tears flow, both of them shaking.

Moments later, Marcy slipped into the room, joining them in their tender, healing moment. For the first time in what felt like an eternity, the three of them felt connected, sharing in the sadness they kept to themselves, and strengthened by the promise of being more open with one another.

17

To

Parker stepped out of his taxi, the sun reflecting off the windshield as he squinted at the rustic wooden sign reading "Long Horn Ranch" in faded white letters. The lake air filled his nostrils, and he could hear the distant sound of waves crashing against the shore. He adjusted his glasses and ran a hand through his messy curls, preparing himself for a week of lifeguard duty at the camp.

"Hey there," called a friendly voice from behind him. Parker turned to see an older man with a salt-and-pepper beard and a sun-weathered face. "You must be Parker. I'm Gus, the head counsellor. Welcome to Long Horn. You'll be joining the other lifeguards at the beach. Just follow the yellow trail; you can't miss it."

"Thanks, Gus," Parker replied, feeling a flutter of nervous excitement in his stomach. He picked up his bag and began making his way down the sandy path, his shoes crunching on the gravel scattered across the ground.

After a few minutes he stumbled onto the beach, Parker's heart skipped a beat when he recognized a familiar figure among the small group of lifeguards. Madison stood there, her brown hair pulled back into a ponytail, a whistle hanging around her neck. Their eyes met, and Parker could feel the tension between them immediately.

"Madison?" Parker said, trying to keep his voice steady. "What are you doing here?"

"Same as you, I guess," she replied, crossing her arms defensively. "Life-guarding for the week."

"Great," Parker muttered under his breath. "So we will be working together the whole week?" the thought made his stomach churn.

"Looks that way," Madison was clearly as unhappy as he was with this development.

Parker looked around at the other lifeguards, "Maybe we won't get the same shifts, you know since there are so many of us,"

"Let's just agree to keep things professional so we can both get through this." Madison returned to the group, but Parker kept a careful distance.

The lifeguard refresher course began, and despite their best efforts, Parker and Madison couldn't help but bicker throughout. They argued over the proper technique for rescuing a drowning swimmer, "Seriously, a fireman's carry, are you nuts!" Madison critiqued as Parker exited the water.

They fought when paired for the CPR training. "Madison, you have to switch off with me at some point! They need to see my technique too," Parker pushed as Madison reached three minutes of consecutive compressions. Somehow, they managed to pass the course, though their already tense relationship was strained further.

———-

Meanwhile, Rodney and his family had just arrived at their hotel room in Disney World, excitement bubbling up as they unpacked their bags. Rodney couldn't wait to check out the park with his sister Marcy.

"Come on, Rod!" Marcy called, her curly hair bouncing as she grabbed her brother's hand. "Let's go explore!"

As they weaved through the throngs of people, riding roller coasters and sharing laughs, Rodney couldn't shake the lingering thought of what it would be like if Parker were there. He knew Parker would appreciate the intricate details of each ride, and they'd quote their favourite movies while waiting in line.

Rodney spotted a guy with messy curls and glasses, so similar to Parker's, he almost walked into a lamp post while staring. He tried to shake the image of Parker out of his head, but it crept back in at every turn. As much fun as he was having with Marcy, he couldn't help but wonder how much more fun it would be with Parker.

"Rodney, you okay?" Marcy asked, noticing his distant expression. "You seem distracted today."

"Uh, yeah. I'm fine," he replied, forcing a smile. But deep down, he realized there wasn't a single moment that day where he thought of Ally, and if he was honest with himself, he didn't really mind that.

———-

The sun cast a golden hue over Long Horn Ranch, as Madison and Parker prepared for their first shared lifeguard shift. They stood side by side, scanning the water, doing their best to pretend the other wasn't there.

"Hey, Madison," Parker began after a full hour of silence, pushing his glasses higher on his nose. "I'm… so sorry about the way it ended between us, you know I didn't want to hurt you? And I can promise you it has nothing to do with Erica." His eyes pleaded with her for forgiveness.

Madison's eyes rolled as she considered his words. "Then who are you really in love with, why did you just lead me on like that?" She hesitated for a moment before continuing. "I just feel used and so confused by everything you did."

Parker exhaled slowly, his gaze lingering on the horizon. "I didn't mean to lead you on, I was just trying so hard to be something I am not," he admitted. "You are amazing and anyone who gets the chance to date you will be so lucky. I just can't love you the way you deserve to be loved, if you get what I am saying."

A wave of sadness washed over Madison's face as she realized what Parker was trying to confess. "Oh Parker, I had no idea… when we go back to school, you need to find out how this mystery person really feels," she advised gently. "Everyone deserves to be happy, and that includes you."

———-

Back at Disney World, Rodney and Marcy strolled through the park, looking for something to eat. As they approached an ice cream stand, Marcy turned to Rodney, concern etched on her freckle-dotted face.

"Hey, how's Ally doing?" she asked. "I haven't really seen her around as often as I used to."

"She's fine," Rodney replied, trying to sound nonchalant. "She's got a boyfriend and she runs a club at school, so she is just a little busy is all."

"Too busy for her best friend?" Marcy said softly. "That doesn't seem like her, we are talking about a girl who blew off her own mother's birthday dinner to come to eat hotdogs with you."

"Hey, I would take a hotdog over a steak any day," Rodney laughed while trying to steer the conversation away from where it was obviously going.

Marcy continued. "Look, all I am saying is people change, and if something has changed between you and Ally, you can tell me about it." She didn't say anything else until they reached the front of the line and she asked "Chocolate or Strawberry?"

As they headed for Space Mountain, Rodney mulled over Marcy's words. He couldn't deny that things had changed between him and Ally, but he wasn't sure what it all meant. Gazing up at the mountain before him, he wondered if he would ever feel the love he had felt for Ally at the beginning of the year again.

———-

Parker lay on his bed in the cabin, moonlight filtering through the window and casting a soft glow across the room. He stared at his phone, scrolling through Rodney's Instagram feed. Pictures of Rodney's adventures over the past year filled the screen - bowling with friends, posing with an enormous ice cream sundae, and even a candid shot of him laughing with Parker while they worked on their French countries project.

As he continued to scroll, Parker thought about how close he and Rodney had grown over the year. He remembered the times he'd caught Rodney giving him a look that made him feel like the center of the universe. The warmth that spread through him at those moments was something he hadn't experienced before, and it both thrilled and terrified him.

His thumb hovered over the message icon, but he hesitated. He wanted to take Madison's advice and ask if Rodney felt the same way he did, but not like this, not through a text. No, it had to be in person, on Monday. A nervous excitement filled his body at the thought of Rodney telling him that he felt the same way. That thought carried Parker off into his dreams.

———-

In Disney World, Rodney approached his mom as she sipped her coffee in the warm Florida sun.

"Hey Mom, can I talk to you about something?" he asked, fidgeting with the hem of his shirt.

"Of course," she replied, setting down her cup. "What's on your mind?"

"I was just wondering… how did you know that Dad was the one?" His voice was hesitant, barely audible above the noise of the bustling theme park.

His mom looked surprised by the question but smiled softly. "Well, at first, I didn't know. Your father was my high school friend, and when he asked me out, I was so afraid it would ruin our friendship that I said no… twice."

Rodney pictured his dad, confident and unyielding despite the rejections, and wished he could have even a fraction of that self-assurance.

"Eventually," she continued, "I said yes, and dating my best friend felt easy. I realized how silly I'd been to say no even once. Love comes naturally when you share a bond of friendship and the same ideals." She studied him for a moment before asking, "Is this about Ally?"

Rodney hesitated, then admitted, "I'm not sure."

———-

The sun began to dip below the horizon, as Parker stood in the cozy cabin, methodically folding his clothes into his duffel bag. He couldn't help but feel a tinge of sadness as he packed up his belongings.

"Hey, Parker," Madison said softly, appearing in the doorway with a sheepish smile. "Just came by to say I had fun this week, despite everything. And… I'd like for us to be friends again."

Parker looked at her, his eyes searching hers before breaking into a genuine smile. "Yeah, me too. I really missed hanging out with you. And thank you for…. understanding."

"Of course," she replied, leaning against the doorframe with a sigh. "So, how are you getting home?"

"Uh, I was planning on taking the bus," Parker admitted, zipping up his bag.

"Want to drive back together? My mom is picking me up. We can maybe make up for some lost time." Madison offered, a hopeful look in her eyes.

"Sounds like a plan," Parker agreed, slinging his bag over his shoulder and following her out of the cabin.

———-

High above the clouds, Rodney gazed out the airplane window, the world below a blur of greens and blues. Marcy sat beside him, fiddling with the cord of her headphones.

"Things have changed between Ally and me," Rodney confessed quietly, staring at the passing clouds. "After Dad died, she was always there. Always trying to include me. It made me feel loved and important to her."

Marcy nodded, listening intently.

"But this year," he continued, "she's just not that person anymore, I'm lucky if I get five minutes with her now. When Dad died, it felt like everyone disappeared from my life but not her. So when she moved all the way here just to ignore me, it hurt so much."

Marcy reached for his hand, giving it a reassuring squeeze. "I know, Rod. But you've changed this year too. You've opened up and made friends on your own - Derek, Parker, Jordan, and Madison. Dad would be proud of you."

He let out a shaky breath, feeling the weight of her words.

"People change and friends come and go," Marcy said softly, her eyes filled with understanding. "But I'll always be here for you." Tears brimmed in Rodney's eyes as he leaned into his sister's embrace, grateful for her unwavering support.

18

Be

Rodney stood at the school entrance, taking a deep breath as he prepared to face another day. His heart raced, feeling the weight of the decision he made over the break. As he stepped inside, he spotted Derek leaning against a row of lockers, engrossed in a novel.

"Hey Derek," Rodney called out, walking towards him with an air of newfound confidence.

Derek looked up and grinned, marking his page before closing the book. "Well, look who's back. How was your break?"

"It was amazing actually," Rodney replied, shuffling his feet. "The first time in a long time we actually had fun as a family. I even have video evidence my mom rode the Tower of Terror"

"Really?" Derek raised an eyebrow, skepticism etched on his face. "I will need to see said video evidence before making my judgment. I am glad that you had a good time, all we did on mine was fish."

"I thought you loved fishing?" Rodney asked, though doubt now lingered in the back of his mind.

"I never said it was a bad thing," Derek said, clapping Rodney on the back. "Now let's walk and talk buddy, because if I am late for Mr. McLellan's class, he's going to sit me in the hallway for sure."

Together, they began walking down the hallway, Rodney was glad to be back talking to Derek, and Marcy was right he had found new friends.

As they turned a corner, they passed by Ally and Matt, who were locked in conversation. Without hesitation, Rodney kept walking, determined not to let his past feelings hold him back.

Ally's eyes widened, surprise etched on her delicate features as she watched Rodney continue down the hall without even stopping.

"Did you just walk by Ally without even a wave?" Derek asked, frowning slightly. "Am I living in Invasion of the Body Snatchers right now?"

"Haha, you are the one who can't be late to class, so I am making sure you get there" Rodney teased, giving a quick glance back toward where Matt and Ally were standing. "I guess I realized Ally has Matt and her own friends. If anything, what this year has taught me is I shouldn't try to force myself to fit into her life and I am fine with that."

"Uh-huh," Derek replied, clearly unconvinced. The bell rang out before he could finish his thought. "Oh crap, I'm late!" he yelled as he disappeared down the hallway.

———-

After school, Rodney made his way to the workout room, driven by his desire to make some changes in his life. He found Matt at the weight bench, lifting an impressive amount of weight. Rodney approached, unsure what to say but knowing that he wanted to finally bury the hatchet.

"Hey, Matt," Rodney began, trying to sound casual. "How was your break?"

Matt grunted, not bothering to look up from his workout. "Fine."

"Listen, I just wanted to clear the air between us." Rodney swallowed hard, feeling vulnerable. "I want you to know that I never wanted to make things complicated between you and Ally. I just wanted to be friends."

Matt finally looked at him, his eyes cold and dismissive. "I don't know what gave you the idea that I cared about what you wanted, I only tolerate you because Ally likes you. So, you go over there and I will stay here and we can both pretend that the other doesn't exist."

"Sorry for bothering you then," Rodney muttered, dejected. He turned to leave, his chest tight and he wondered why Matt's words hurt him so much. He knew Matt didn't like him but this still felt like a knife to the heart. He decided he could start working out another day and fled the room.

———-

Rodney's sneakers scuffed against the sidewalk, the weight of Matt's rejection still heavy on his shoulders. He tugged at the strap of his backpack, inhaling sharply in an attempt to keep his emotions in check.

"Hey, Rodney!" Derek called out, jogging over to him. "I thought you were planning on working out, you know to 'start fresh after the break' as you put it. What happened?"

"I ran into Matt. I should have known he would be there, he practically lives there. I probably shouldn't have tried to talk to him, but I did and it blew up in my face," Rodney admitted, his voice wavering slightly as he recounted the events that unfolded in the workout room.

"What did that idiot say?" Derek's face darkened, and his fists clenched. "Do I need to find him and teach him a lesson?"

"Thanks, but I was the one who went over there and talked to him." Rodney forced a weak smile. "I can't blame him for not liking me, from his perspective I have been all over his girlfriend for months. I just hope over time he can see I really just want to hang out with my friend without it feeling like she's cheating"

"Wow, so you did go on some kind of spirit quest over break or something? Did Mufasa appear to you in the stars?" Derek teased, but his eyes remained serious. "Look at you, all mature and stuff."

"Something like that." Rodney shrugged. "But right now all I want is a BBQ chicken pizza and a smoothie."

"Ah, now there is the Rodney I know," Derek replied. "Let's get you that pizza." They both laughed and headed off down the road to Pepi's Pizza.

———-

The week passed by quickly and Friday night finally rolled around, Rodney kicked off his shoes when he got home and noticed his mom was doing a double shift and Marcy was out with friends, so he would be home alone tonight.

His phone buzzed, "I just got Until Dawn, want to play it?" Parker texted, nervous energy radiating from the phone.

"Sounds good to me," Rodney agreed, "My place is empty if you want to come here."

"Awesome see you soon" In no time at all Parker walked through the front door.

"Right this way" Rodney motioned Parker inside. "I have the PS4 all setup and ready to go."

The pair made their way to the living room and found their positions on the couch. Parker slipped in the game and watched the intro all about how the choices they make will impact the story later on.

"This is going to be fun," Rodney said, his face lighting up with anticipation. Parker looked at Rodney just glowing and felt lucky just to be there. Parker nodded in agreement and the game began.

As the night wore on, Parker's heart hammered in his chest. Rodney had seemed to not mind that he moved closer to him, and he could feel the weight of the words he had always wanted to say pressing against his lips. Rodney leaned forward, eyes focused on the screen, blissfully unaware of the internal storm brewing within his friend.

"Rodney," Parker practically shouted, startling them both. He paused the game, hands shaking as he gripped the controller. "There's something I need to tell you."

"Uh sure, what's up?" Rodney asked, eyebrows furrowing with concern. Unsure why Parker had taken such a serious tone all of a sudden.

Taking a deep breath, Parker confessed, "I really like you. And not just, like, as a friend. More like in an, I want to kiss you kind of way." Parker's face went beet red, but he knew Madison's advice was right and he needed to know.

Rodney blinked, clearly taken aback. "Wait, what? Are you serious?" Rodney searched Parker's eyes for any signs of deception, cautiously aware this could be a joke.

"Dead serious," Parker replied, his voice wavering slightly. "I've never felt this way about a guy before, or anyone for that matter, and I don't even know if you're into guys or not. I was so scared of ruining our friendship that I didn't say anything. Plus, I knew how you felt about Ally, and I didn't want to get in the way…."

Before Parker could continue his thought spiral, Rodney burst into laughter.

"You are starting to sound just like me. In all honesty though for the entire break, the only person I wanted to be there with was you. Fair warning I've never kissed anyone before, but I wouldn't mind giving it a try with you." he blushed.

"Really?" Parker's face lit up, as he looked into Rodney's eyes.

"Absolutely," Rodney confirmed, a grin spreading across his face.

With a shared glance, they leaned in, their lips meeting in a tentative kiss. At that moment, Rodney's mind filled with fireworks, sparks igniting like the grand finale of a fairy tale. When they pulled apart, they stared at each other, breathless.

"Wow," Rodney whispered, his cheeks flushed. "How did that feel for you?"

"It was great, way better than any other kiss I have had," Parker breathed, his eyes shining with happiness. "You?"

"I literally saw fireworks," Rodney said, he had thought about kissing Parker so many times before now, and now that he had, he wished he had done it sooner.

They leaned in for another kiss, this one more passionate and lingering. But as they lost themselves in each other's embrace, the sound of a knock at the door brought them back to reality. They sprang apart just as Parker's dad was waiting at the front door.

"Hey, boys," he shouted through the door, oblivious to their previous actions. "Parker your phone must be dead, I didn't hear back from you."

"Uh, oh yeah it must have died without me noticing," Parker called back, getting up to answer the door.

"Well, it is almost curfew, time for me to take you home," Parker's father informed them as they opened the door.

"Sorry about that," Rodney added, trying to appear casual. "We totally lost track of time."

"I get it, boys will be boys. Grab your game and hop in the car, let's go," With that, Parker's dad left to wait in the beat-up Ford Fiesta, closing the door behind him.

"Rodney," Parker began hesitantly, his gaze flicking away from his friend, "Can we keep this a secret? It's just you know how crazy catholic my dad is, he would kick me out for sure if he found out."

"Of course," Rodney agreed, understanding the concern etched on Parker's face. "I don't want you to get hurt over a kiss. And honestly, I don't know how my mom would feel about it either,"

"Thank you," Parker whispered, relief washing over him as he reached for Rodney's hand. The two smiled softly at each other, but Rodney wondered in the back of his mind if he really could keep this amazing thing a secret forever.

———-

As the car vanished around the corner, Rodney thought about Parker, the way he smiled, the way the kiss felt, how he wished he could feel that way forever. The sky was a blend of rich purples and blues, dotted with stars that seemed to wink at him as he stared up at them.

Rodney flopped onto his bed, his phone buzzing in his pocket. He pulled it out to find a text from Derek. "Hey man," it read, "How did the gaming go?"

Rodney hesitated, his thumbs hovering over the screen. Part of him wanted to tell Derek everything - about Parker saying he liked him as more than a friend and their Earth-shattering kiss. But he remembered the vulnerability in Parker's eyes when he'd asked to keep their kiss a secret, and Rodney didn't want to betray that trust. Besides, he wasn't sure how Derek would react to the news. Would Derek hate him if he knew he liked another guy? Rodney didn't want to find out the answer to that question.

"Pretty laid back, actually," he typed, trying to keep his response casual. "Just hung out with Parker and played video games."

"Sounds chill," Derek replied. "You should come over this weekend and play the newest Dark Pictures game with me. It's supposed to be intense!"

Rodney's stomach twisted into knots at the thought of spending time with Derek while keeping such a monumental secret. What if he accidentally let something slip? He couldn't risk losing both of his friends over this.

"I will if I have time," he wrote back. "I've got a mountain of homework to tackle."

"Ah, bummer," came Derek's response. "Well, let me know if you want to hang out later this week. Later, dude!"

"Will do. Later!" Rodney sent one last message before putting his phone away. He felt guilty lying to Derek, Derek was his friend after all, and real friends don't just stop being your friend over something as small as who you like. Rodney tried to convince himself of this fact, but a voice in the back of his mind whispered that telling anyone would cause him more harm than good.

19

Happy

The dim glow of the television illuminated the cozy scene on the couch in Rodney's living room. Rodney and Parker were snuggled together under a warm blanket, Monster's Inc. playing on the screen. Rodney couldn't help but feel his heart swell with happiness as he revelled in this rare alone time with Parker. They had been together a month, but it still didn't feel real to Rodney.

"Hey," Parker whispered, a mischievous glint in his eyes as he turned to face Rodney. The corners of his mouth curled up into a grin as he leaned in, capturing Rodney's lips with his own. Just as they began to lose themselves in the passion of the moment, the shrill sound of an incoming FaceTime call pierced through the air.

"Shit! I forgot I told Derek I would Facetime him tonight and play COD." Rodney muttered, disentangling himself from Parker's embrace. "I have to take this," he said apologetically, rushing out of the room to answer the call.

"Hey, Derek," he answered, trying to keep his voice steady as he lied. "I am so sorry, I'm watching a movie with Mom tonight, you know to help us reconnect."

"Really?" Derek asked, raising an eyebrow. "But you told me Marcy and your mom were away at her dance competition this weekend."

"Uh, yeah," Rodney stammered, thinking quickly. "The competition got cancelled last minute. They came back early."

"Ah, that's too bad," Derek replied, clearly believing Rodney's lie. "Well, hopefully we can hang out later then?"

"Definitely," Rodney agreed, relieved that Derek hadn't caught him in the lie. "Talk to you later, man." in his haste to get back to Parker, he hung up on Derek before Derek could say goodbye. A strange guilt filled his body, it was getting easier to lie to Derek and he wasn't sure if that was a good thing.

"Rodney! Come back!" Parker called from the living room, his voice carrying a playful tone. Rodney couldn't help but smile as he rejoined Parker on the couch, the guilt melting away as he snuggled up once more to enjoy the rest of their movie night.

———-

On Monday, Rodney sat down for lunch with Derek as usual. "Hey, so there's a new skate park that just got installed in Victoria Park. Wanna check it out later?" Derek asked, taking a bite of his sandwich.

"Uh," Rodney hesitated, mentally cursing himself for making plans with Parker later that day. He realised he was becoming just as flaky as Ally was, now that he had a secret boyfriend. "I can't today, man. I have to catch up on some chores I put off over the weekend."

"Really?" Derek frowned, clearly disappointed. "Man, I am beginning to feel like you have a secret best friend I don't know about."

Overhearing their conversation, Madison slid into the seat next to them, her curiosity piqued. "Are you seeing someone in secret, Rodney?" she asked, her eyes narrowing playfully.

"What no Derek was just…" Rodney started.

"Whoever it is must be pretty special if you're lying to your best friend," Derek chimed in, feigning sadness.

"Guys, it's not like that," Rodney protested weakly, feeling the heat rise to his cheeks. Why was this happening now, he had worked so hard, and faked so many illnesses, if it came out like this what would Parker do? They would break up for sure Rodney thought.

"Relax," Derek said, seeing Rodney's horrified expression. "We are just giving you a hard time. But if a mystery person is trying to get friendly with you, remind them the position of best friend has been taken,"

"No argument there," Rodney agreed, knowing full well he'd have to tell Derek eventually. As Madison rattled off guesses as to who Rodney's secret lover could be, all of which Rodney denied, he couldn't help but feel a mix of happiness and dread. He was thrilled to finally feel free with Parker, but he didn't feel fully free, maybe it was because he couldn't share this happiness with the other people he cared about.

———-

After school, Rodney found himself crossing paths with Ally in the hallway. She seemed to have been waiting for him, pacing in a small circle by his locker.

"Hey, Rodney," she said, falling into step beside him. "I couldn't help but overhear your lunch conversation earlier. So, you're seeing someone?"

Rodney tensed up, feeling like a deer caught in headlights. He tried to play it cool, shrugging nonchalantly. "No, is just Derek being Derek, and you know Madison, she is always trying to find some good gossip."

Ally studied him for a moment, taking in his flushed cheeks and the way he avoided her gaze. It was clear that Rodney was hiding something, and it stirred an unexpected hurt that he wouldn't just tell her. She found herself questioning if their friendship had really been strained to the point where Rodney kept secrets from her.

"Right, well if you aren't too busy, I'm having a party next Saturday, I would love to see you there," she said softly, offering him a smile before walking away before he could answer, her mind consumed by the idea that Rodney may not need her anymore.

———-

Meanwhile, Parker was practically floating through the hallways, his happiness radiating off of him. His recent A+ on his math test only made him feel better, to him life was perfect.

"Alright, Parker, you can't keep this secret any longer," Steven declared during their afternoon hangout in the school courtyard. Luke nodded in agreement, his curiosity piqued by Parker's newfound joy.

"Why are you so happy all of a sudden? Who did this to you?" Luke asked, his eyes narrowing playfully.

Parker shook his head, a mischievous grin on his face. "What can I say, I am killing it recently, that's all."

"Ah, come on!" Steven feigned hurt, clutching at his heart dramatically. "We're supposed to be friends, man! Friends don't keep secrets from each other," he added with a wink.

Laughing, Parker glanced around to make sure no one was listening in. "I know, I know. But a true gentleman doesn't kiss and tell," he said.

Luke and Steven exchanged glances "What a tease," they said in unions, deciding to let the matter rest for now. They couldn't deny how happy Parker seemed, and that was good enough for them.

But as they joked and laughed, Parker's thoughts kept drifting back to Rodney. He felt a warmth in his chest that he hadn't experienced before, a happiness that seemed to grow with every stolen moment they shared. In his mind, everything was absolutely perfect.

———-

Friday night Parker stood outside the entrance of Silvercity, his heart fluttering with anticipation as he waited for Rodney to climb out of the back seat. A sudden gust of wind sent a shiver down his spine, causing him to pull his jacket tighter around himself.

"Sorry about the wait, my shoe got caught on the middle thing," Rodney explained, standing next to Parker with a smile that seemed to light up the gloomy evening.

"No worries, I don't know how many times I have gotten caught on that thing," Parker replied, returning the smile. He could sense the nervous energy radiating off Rodney, as they both waited for Parker's dad to leave. Before Parker's dad pulled away, he rolled down the window with a stern look on his face.

"Make sure you boys see something manly, alright?" he said, eyeing them suspiciously. "Don't want people getting the wrong idea about you two."

"Of course, Dad," Parker assured him, cringing internally at the comment. "We're going to watch Mission Impossible. It's action-packed and everything."

"Alright then," Parker's father said, nodding in approval, "Text me when you need a ride home." With that, he drove off into the night, leaving the two boys to navigate the crowded lobby.

"Let's get our tickets before it gets too packed," Rodney suggested, pulling Parker towards the ticket booth. They exchanged a knowing glance as they purchased their tickets for The Greatest Showman instead of Mission Impossible, as they had promised.

"Are you ready for this?" Parker asked, squeezing Rodney's hand as they slipped into the dimly lit theatre. The atmosphere inside was electric, with excited theatre-goers chattering and finding their seats.

"More than ready," Rodney whispered back, this was their first date outside of Rodney's house, and Rodney couldn't be more excited for it. As the lights dimmed and the musical began, Parker couldn't help but sing along to each song, his voice soft and surprisingly melodic.

"Through the dark, through the door," he sang under his breath, his eyes fixed on the screen. Rodney watched him with a growing sense of wonder, realizing that he found Parker's enthusiasm absolutely adorable. Parker had always been smart and kind, but for Rodney, he just seemed to get smarter and kinder with every passing moment.

As the final notes of the show rang out and the audience erupted into applause, Rodney impulsively leaned over and pressed a gentle kiss to Parker's lips. It was simple, pure but it took Parker by surprise, he pulled away but only for a moment before returning the kiss.

"Wow," Parker whispered as they pulled away, his cheeks flushed with delight. "What was that for?"

"For being you," Rodney replied, his heart pounding in his ears. "I think I lo...." Rodney started to say but then he remembered they were in a crowded movie theatre where anyone could hear them.

The words hung between them, both surprised about how close Rodney had been to saying the one thing they both wanted to hear. Parker's eyes widened, and for a moment, he thought about finishing Rodney's sentence for him. But as he looked into Rodney's earnest gaze, he reminded himself that his dad would never let them actually be together.

"Rodney," he murmured, his voice thick with emotion. "I think... I think we should head so my dad doesn't get too suspicious." the two boys left the theatre in awkward silence.

The night air was cool on their flushed cheeks as they stepped out of the theatre, both of them chastising themselves for messing up the night.

"Thanks for the amazing date," Rodney said, casting a sideways glance at Parker, trying to revive the joy he had felt earlier in the night.

"Anyhow, I've been listening to the soundtrack on a loop," Parker replied, his eyes sparkling with enthusiasm. "I'm glad you enjoyed it too."

As Parker's dad pulled up to the curb, he rolled down the window and gave them a scrutinizing look. "You boys have a good time?"

"Absolutely, sir," Rodney responded, trying his best to sound convincing. Parker's dad nodded, and they climbed into the backseat, their fingertips grazing each other but never connecting.

It wasn't a long drive back to Parker's house, but it felt like an eternity as they sat in silence, unable to discuss the night's events. When the car finally pulled up to the front of Parker's house, Parker offered to walk Rodney home.

"Really, it's no trouble," Parker insisted, brushing off Rodney's protests. "Besides, I could use the fresh air."

Under the starlit sky, they walked side by side, unsure of what they should say to each other. "So, my family is going away to my grandma's next weekend. I am sure I can get out of it if I fake sick. Would you want to come over and keep me company?" Parker suggested.

"Yeah, that would be awesome," Rodney whispered, feeling like his slip-up didn't ruin the whole night.

When they reached Rodney's front door, Parker hesitated for a moment before leaning in and pressing a tender kiss to Rodney's lips. "Goodnight, Rodney," he murmured, his breath warm against Rodney's cheek.

"Goodnight, Parker," Rodney replied, wishing he could get another kiss before Parker left. He watched Parker walk away, and Rodney wondered why the L word was so hard for him to say when he wanted to say it so badly.

Rodney turned the doorknob and entered his house, only to find Derek waiting for him in the living room. Surprise washed over Rodney's face as his brain scrambled to come up with an explanation.

"Hey, I came by to see if you wanted to catch a movie," Derek said, raising an eyebrow. "But your mom told me they were already at the movies. And I didn't mean to see your private moment but I kind of did, we don't have to talk about it though."

Rodney could feel the heat creeping up his neck, but he managed a sheepish smile. "Yeah, about that… I'm sorry I didn't tell you right away. I wanted to tell, I have wanted to tell you for weeks now, but I just couldn't."

Derek leaned back, a silly grin spreading across his face. "I get it, not everyone would be cool with it, the last thing you need are idiots making a big deal out of it. But Rodney, buddy, do I look like an idiot to you?"

Taking a deep breath, Rodney laughed, "No, I was just overthinking it. And while we are on the topic of overthinking, I think I'm in love with Parker. I've never felt this way before, so I don't know for sure, but when I am with him, it is like nothing else in the world exists."

A warm smile spread across Derek's face. "Sounds like love to me, man. Have you told him any of this?"

"I want to," Rodney agreed, "but every time I try, I freeze up. I think about everything that could go wrong and what would happen if his dad found out and it just feels like a lot,"

"You don't have to announce it to the entire world," Derek explained, grinning. "You need some kind of romantic moment where you can just tell him how you feel."

Rodney's eyes lit up. "You think so?"

"Of course, it is all about setting the right mood," Derek said, clapping Rodney on the shoulder. "I am sure we can figure out a perfect way to get you and Parker alone and in the mood to confess those feelings." Rodney nodded, hoping that with Derek's help, he would finally be able to say what he wanted to.

20

Again.

The sun beat down on the school as students spilled out onto the front lawn, chatting excitedly about their summer plans. The scent of freshly cut grass mingled with anticipation in the air; it was the time of year when everyone was counting down the final days of school.

Rodney stood by his locker, eyes fixed on Ally as Matt approached her with a bouquet the size of a small garden. As he asked her to the spring formal, her cheeks flushed pink, and she grinned widely, accepting the invitation with a nod. Rodney felt a little envious as he watched the scene play out, but he tried to suppress it as he turned back to Marcy and Derek talking animatedly nearby. They had agreed to go to the dance together as friends, a fact that Marcy had drilled into Derek, with a particular stress on the word friend.

"Hey," Parker greeted, appearing at Rodney's side and snapping him out of his thoughts. "Ready for class?"

"Uh, yeah, sure," Rodney stammered, as he met those deep brown eyes behind the glasses he wondered if they would ever be able to go to a dance together as a couple.

"By the way," Parker added, leaning closer to Rodney, so only he could hear, "I have a surprise for you after school."

"Really?" Rodney's mind raced at the possibilities – was this it? Was Parker actually going to ask him to the spring formal or tell him he loved him? He spent the rest of the day lost in elaborate fantasies of how Parker could emerge with the school band to deliver his confession of love.

———-

After school Rodney met Parker out by the football stands, "Close your eyes," Parker instructed, standing before Rodney in the deserted field.

"Okay…" Rodney complied, feeling both nervous and excited.

"Open them."

Before Rodney's eyes lay a delicate silver chain with a tiny glow-in-the-dark firefly pendant dangling from it. He gasped in awe but couldn't help feeling a twinge of disappointment that it wasn't a confession of love or an invite to the dance.

"I saw it in the store and thought of you since you light up my life," Parker said, his voice sincere and filled with emotion.

"Thank you, Parker. I love it," Rodney managed to say, though his heart ached as he realized he would have to lie about how he got it to all their friends. Taking a deep breath, he decided to try. He would have to be the one to nudge their relationship a little further. He wanted that moment where they could tell each other how they really felt. "Parker, will you go to the semi-formal with me?"

Parker hesitated for a moment, clearly worried about the implications of attending the dance together. "As friends?" he asked cautiously.

"Of course, as friends," Rodney reassured him, masking his sadness as best he could. "No one has to know we're a thing."

"Okay then," Parker agreed, relief evident in his eyes. "As friends."

Rodney leaned in to kiss Parker softly on the lips, but he pulled away hearing students approaching. Parker smiled and hurried away, Rodney couldn't help but glance down at the firefly pendant in his hand, a bittersweet reminder that their love remained hidden from the world.

———-

The next day at school, Rodney found himself in the bustling ticket line for the spring formal, this year's theme was enchanted garden. With a mixture of excitement and anxiety, he swayed in line. He clutched the money tightly in his hand, listening to his peers discussing how they asked their partners to the dance. He wondered why it seemed so easy for everyone else to talk about their relationships.

"Hey, Rodney!" Madison's voice cut through the chatter as she pushed her way into the line, her eyes bright with curiosity. "Are those tickets for you and your mystery girlfriend?"

Rodney felt a flush creep up his neck as he hastily denied it. "No, I don't have a girlfriend. Parker and I are just going as friends."

Madison tilted her head, a knowing glint in her eyes as she studied Rodney's expression. The gears spinning in her mind as she put two and two together. She pressed her tongue to the roof of her mouth, unwilling to expose something so personal without permission.

"Alright," she conceded, her tone cautious yet teasing. "Well, I am looking forward to seeing you and Parker at the dance. It's a big night so maybe some big things will happen,"

"Maybe," Rodney said, though a part of him wondered if Parker wanted anything to change at all. He met her gaze and realized the sadness that had spread across his own.

Madison nodded solemnly, taking the unspoken plea to heart. "Look Rodney I know I am the queen of gossip, it is who I am, but I would never break the seal on something like this, ok? Just enjoy the dance, no pressure."

"Thanks, Madison," Rodney murmured, grateful for her understanding. She left with a reassuring smile, leaving him to grapple with the fact more and more people seemed to be figuring it out even without them telling anyone.

As the day wore on, Rodney couldn't shake the feeling that he was in over his head. He loved Parker, but why hadn't either of them said it out loud? Was it the fear of being outed, or something deeper? He thought about Steven and Jordan, who seemed so at ease with themselves and each other. Would things be easier if they were open about their feelings? Would being out fix the uncertainty he was feeling in the relationship? All these questions began to give Rodney a serious headache.

———-

That evening, as Rodney and Parker walked hand-in-hand through the dimly lit paths of Victoria Park, he decided to tackle the issue head-on. "Parker," he began hesitantly, "should we come out to our friends?"

Parker's grip tightened around Rodney's hand, his expression clouding over with uncertainty. "No," he replied firmly. "We're not gay. We're just having fun, and that's nobody's business but our own."

"I never said we were gay, I just feel like there is so much I want to talk about with them, you know. Like, I would like to tell them how my amazing boyfriend bought me the Firefly chain and not that I bought it for myself. I mean don't you want to talk to your friends about me too?"

"Of course I do, Rodney, but they just wouldn't get it. This thing we have is so special and sharing it with them would just make it a little less special." Parker seemed desperate to get Rodney to see things the way he did.

"I mean I guess you could be right, but Steven is with Jordan, and no one seems to care. I just wish I could at least stop lying to them, it is making me feel guilty," Rodney admitted.

"They are fine and everything is perfect as is," Parker stated.

Rodney's heart sank at the dismissal, but he nodded in agreement, unwilling to push Parker further away. They continued their walk through the park, but their conversation had come to a complete standstill.

———-

The night of the Spring formal had finally arrived, and Rodney felt a mixture of excitement and anxiety as he stared at his reflection in the mirror. He did up the final buttons on one of his dad's old dress shirts, which fit him perfectly after he rolled up the sleeves and tucked it in. He checked himself out in the mirror, feeling like he was ready to take on the world.

"Wow, you look so much like your father," his mother said from the doorway, her eyes welling up with tears. "I hope tonight is amazing for you, sweetheart."

"Thanks, Mom," Rodney replied, wrapping her in a tight embrace. He could feel her love in the tight hug, they still had their issues, but things were getting better.

When he arrived at Parker's house, however, he found his date wearing a casual outfit, his breath smelled like alcohol. Rodney tried not to let his disappointment show, but it was difficult when he had been looking forward to sharing this special evening with Parker. "Do you need more time to get ready?" he asked, trying to sound nonchalant.

"No, I'm good to go," Parker slurred, swaying slightly on his feet. With a sigh, Rodney took Parker's arm to steady him and led him to the Uber.

"Did you really need to drink before the dance?" Rodney asked, concern lacing his voice.

"Needed to loosen up, be fun," Parker mumbled, avoiding eye contact.

"Everyone thinks we are going as friends, there really is nothing to worry about," Rodney couldn't help but wonder if it was less about having fun and more about Parker's fear of being outed.

"I am not worried, and I am more fun this way anyway. Now let's go rock this thing!" Parker said, louder than he should have.

As they entered the dance, Rodney spotted Jordan and Steven in matching suits, grinning broadly as they waved them over. Steven's eyes narrowed with concern as he noticed Parker's intoxicated state. "He looks awful, how did he even get through the doors?"

"Well, Ms. McMansion is manning the door it is no wonder he got in, the woman is pushing ninety," Jordan responded, looking a Parker with concern.

"I'll take him to get some food and water, sober him up a bit" Steven offered, leading Parker away. Rodney watched them go and wondered if Parker had gotten so drunk in hopes they would be turned away at the door.

"Where's Parker?" Derek asked as he and Marcy joined Rodney on the dance floor.

"Steven's trying to sober him up. Parker was drinking before we got here," Rodney explained, trying to keep his voice steady despite his worry.

"Are you okay?" Derek inquired, placing a hand on Rodney's shoulder. "I know you were looking forward to this night."

"I just... I feel like I put too much pressure on him to come to the dance," Rodney confessed, his gaze downcast. "Like maybe he thought something was going to happen that wasn't,"

"Hey," Marcy interjected gently, "I am not sure what is going on here, but you didn't do anything wrong. It sounds like Parker isn't in a good place is all."

"What do you mean?" Rodney asked, looking up at her.

"We all do stupid things when we don't feel great about something or feel pressure, but getting wasted was his choice. He could have just told you he didn't want to come but he chose not to and that isn't your fault." Marcy explained, her eyes filled with understanding.

Rodney shook his head, unwilling to accept her words. "No, I basically forced him here. I have to find him." He realized he may have just spilled the secret to Marcy, but he didn't care anymore, he had to let Parker know how he really felt.

When Rodney finally tracked down Steven, he received the heartbreaking news "Sorry buddy, Parker left. He called an Uber and just headed out. I was going to tell you when I found you" Steven admitted. The words crashed over Rodney like a tidal wave, and he felt like he was being pulled under, surrounded by laughter and music that only seemed to suck the life out of him. Parker didn't even try to tell him he was leaving, Parker didn't tell him he didn't want to go to the dance and Parker never told him he loved him.

———-

Rodney's heart ached, the weight of Parker's absence crushing him as he slipped out of the dance and into the night air. He found himself drawn to the school garden, a sanctuary that had once sheltered him during the fall formal. Moonlight bathed the familiar bench where he had met Derek, and Rodney sank down onto it, feeling lost and alone.

Tears streamed down his cheeks as he replayed the night in his mind, wondering if there was something he could have done differently. Was it too much to hope that he could finally tell Parker he loved him? His heart clenched at the thought, and he struggled to breathe, feeling suffocated by his own emotions. With trembling fingers, he removed his bowtie and stuffed it into his pocket, desperate for some relief from the tightness that seemed to constrict his chest.

"Rodney?" The voice was soft, concerned, and so achingly familiar.

"Ally," he choked out, surprised to see her standing there in the moonlit garden, her royal blue dress shimmering like water beneath the stars.

"Are you okay?" Ally asked gently, taking a seat beside him on the bench.

"I don't know," he admitted, wiping away tears with the back of his hand. "I just... I feel so stupid."

"Hey, don't say that. You're not stupid, Rodney." Ally reached over, placing a comforting hand on his shoulder. "Talk to me. What happened?"

"Things didn't go so well with my date," Rodney said, swallowing the lump in his throat. "They got drunk and left me here at the dance."

"Rodney, I'm so sorry," Ally murmured, her eyes filled with empathy. "You deserve so much better."

"Thanks, Ally," he whispered, offering her a weak smile as he tried to pull himself together. He then noticed Ally's own tear-stricken face.

"Are you ok? Shouldn't you be in there enjoying the dance with Matt?" he asked, wondering what led her out into the night.

"No, I don't think we will be dancing with each other anytime soon. Let's just say we had a… disagreement about where our relationship was headed," Ally replied, her voice carrying a note of sadness. "I realized I was trying to help someone – who honestly didn't want my help."

"I'm sorry," Rodney said, as they both sat down on the bench. "You deserve someone amazing, Ally."

"Thanks, Rodney," she smiled, leaning her head on his shoulder as they sat in companionable silence, two bruised hearts finding solace in the moonlit garden.

After a few minutes, their eyes met, and Ally's hand found his. Rodney shifted on the bench, unsure of what exactly was happening here, He looked down at her, "Ally I think…"

She pressed her finger to his lips to silence him, "Rodney for once can you just not think too much about things," she whispered, moving her lips closer to his. They met in the darkness, creating a kiss Rodney had waited years for.

Rodney felt guilt wash over him as he thought about what Parker would think about the kiss, but at the same time kissing Ally was what he wanted for so long and it felt so comforting.

Ally didn't know what she wanted, but she did know that she wanted Rodney back in her life and this felt like a way to do that. Neither of them knew what would come next, or whether they were making the right choice, but in that moment none of it mattered.